BILLY BONES: A TALE FROM THE SECRETS CLOSET

Christopher Lincoln

GALAXY

PLUS

First published in Great Britain
by Macmillan Children's Books,
a division of
Macmillan Publishers Ltd, 2008
This Large Print edition published by
BBC Audiobooks
by arrangement with
Macmillan Children's Books 2008

ISBN: 978 1405 662802

British Library Cataloguing in Publication Data available

Printed and bound in Great Britain by
Antony Rowe Ltd., Chippenham, Wiltshire

For my children

PROLOGUE

BASIC GUIDE TO THE AFTERLIFE

By Porticleese Longbone, Secretary of Reception

Welcome to the Afterlife. And as we Afterlifers are fond of saying, 'May your eternity not feel like one.'

As your last sparks of mortality wink out, I might suggest, this is the perfect time to review a few basics. Hopefully you'll find this guide helpful as you ready yourself for judgement and placement procedures.

Please note: This guide focuses on the Light Side of the Afterlife. Information about the Dark Side is available in their receiving department (if you are unlucky enough to be heading that way).

If you've just picked this booklet up, you must be standing in the Hall of Reception. And you have no doubt met Mr Grim Bones. (Perhaps he's reading over your shoulder right now?) Most people on Earth know him as the Angel of Death or the Grim Reaper. It's his duty to collect you and guide you through the hallways connecting your previous world to this one, the Afterlife.

Looking around, you might be thinking, *Most of these Afterlifers are skeletons.* But calm your bubbling fears—no, you are not going to suddenly transform into a skeleton. The Afterlife is full of normal souls, just like you.

You are seeing so many skeletons because you are in the Hall of Reception, one of the Afterlife

1

departments managed by skeletons. The other is the Department of Fibs and Fabrications. Ghostly spirits staff all other departments (except for those in the Dark Side; those offices employ other strange and detestable creatures).

GOVERNMENT OF THE AFTERLIFE

The Afterlife government has two branches, the Righteousness Department for the Light Side and the Department of Injustice for the Dark. Both these branches report to the Realms Above, and have many sub-departments. I won't bore you by listing them (even with all eternity, that would take too long).

I will, however, tell you about one: the Department of Fibs and Fabrications.

You might be surprised to learn that for much of your life, skeletons were close by. You see, everyone has a skeleton or two in their closet. When you were just a baby, first forming words, the Department of Fibs and Fabrications was already selecting your secrets-closet skeletons. These dedicated workers keep track of your lies and secrets and pack them away into storage.

Lies and secrets are both ways of hiding truth. Lies are simply falsehoods and secrets are hidden truths. But be warned: both will flare up in the light of truth. The blacker the lie and the darker the secret, the more severe the explosion.

Secrets-closet skeletons know not to store lies and secrets in a jumble. They must be sorted and packed carefully into trunks. The Department of Fibs and Fabrications, or the DFF, keeps close tabs on the various ways people shroud truth, and DFF skeletons aren't the only ones interested. There is quite an interest in the Realms Above. Keeping track of these sorts of things is how they pass judgement for your Afterlife placement.

You might be wondering now, what if a human enters a secrets closet? To this date, due to our many procedures and teams of dedicated skeletons, that has thankfully never happened.

GHOSTS VS SKELETONS

Ghosts come in a number of varieties, like wraiths, poltergeists, phantasms and banshees. But most keep translucent versions of the bodies they left behind.

Skeletons can live effortlessly on Earth, but ghosts find it tiring and must visit the Afterlife every so often to recover. Most ghosts think they're above all that 'earthly nonsense'—they never miss a chance to look down on skeletons.

Not everyone on Earth can see ghosts. But they can see skeletons, so it's important for skeletons to keep to their closets, and for couriers to travel in darkest night.

MANIFESTATIONS

Perhaps the most curious residents of the Afterlife are manifestations. These beings are cut from the brighter and darker cloths of the human heart.

The Goods are physical manifestations of qualities like Bravery, Dedication, Trust and

Selflessness. When the Goods travel to Earth, they are locked inside your heart, which is why you rarely see them. But once on Earth, a heart can be tempted by the Bads. These are the darker manifestations, like Pride, Anger and Greed. They are fiercely hungry, so watch out for them, even here in the Afterlife! They have many brothers: regrettably, they number in the millions. They riddle the heart of anyone unwise enough to let them in. But it's hard to spot them unless you have a talent for seeing what ought not to be there.

YOUR FIRST DAY IN THE GREAT BEYOND

After you have been escorted out of the Hall of Reception, what's next?

Well, pretty much whatever your heart desires. Most new arrivals receive a life-after-lifetime supply of golden wishes (the currency of the Afterlife). Use these wishes to create anything at all, from shooting-star roller coasters to chocolate and Big Dipper ice cream to the home you remember on Earth. You can also use your wishes to transport yourself from one place to another. But be careful: even though you have a vast supply of wishes, it *is* possible to spend them all.

Now, get out there, find your assigned section of the Afterlife and start building those castles in the air. Explore and enjoy. After all, you've been waiting a lifetime.

Part 1

LIVING IN DARKNESS

In darkness all the lies lie hid
Upon them you can put a lid
But fear this: at some future time
They'll be exposed to light divine

CHAPTER 1

THE SECRETS CLOSET

Shadows upon shadows—that's what greeted Billy when he opened his eyes. It was another dark morning. Mornings, afternoons and evenings were always dark where Billy lived. He whisked back his spiderweb curtain and hopped out of the old chest that served as his bed.

Clickety-thunk. His bony feet hit the creaky floor. Billy's mum looked up with a warm smile. Smiles were common in the Bones family, as common as a kettle in any other family.

'You're looking thin and pale,' Mrs Bones observed, 'even for a skeleton. Someday we'll get you outside to play.'

'Someday,' sighed his dad, shaking his head.

Mr Bones sat just behind his wife with an old pipe jammed in his mouth. He rumpled his newspaper and continued reading—the same newspaper he had been reading all week. Not much changed in the Boneses' world.

7

Their residence was a dark and tightly locked closet, filled with jumbled piles of family secrets. Billy and his parents lived among boxed-up lies, hidden misfortunes and horrid half-truths, the kind no family would ever want aired in public. The closet was locked away in High Manners Manor, a monstrous hilltop estate belonging to the Biglum family, a proud family held in the highest esteem by their well-to-do neighbours.

Billy was as tall as a ten-year-old and wasn't angular and mean like many closet skeletons. He was a dreamer and liked a good hug. His eyes were the palest blue and had a softness about them. Contrary to popular opinion, skeletons, particularly secrets-closet skeletons, have light-filled, luminous eyes—not empty eye sockets. They also wear clothes, although Billy's were in a dreadful state of tatters. Mrs Bones tried her best, but clothes from the Afterlife were in such short supply. Billy's shirt had been surrendered to the rag pile years earlier. Most days he dressed in only a pair of ragged shorts and socks.

Mrs Bones wore a shawl, a bonnet and not much more, except a gentle smile. Mr Bones's wardrobe was a herringbone jacket and, occasionally, a cap.

*   *   *

Billy's parents, Lars and Decette Bones, doted on him as much as they could, locked away in their stuffy closet home.

Skeletons don't need much to survive. As you can imagine, eating is out of the question. Breathing? Not necessary. Nor is bathing. Really all that a skeleton needs to survive is a simple secrets closet and maybe a family member or two.

But Billy's desires ran in another direction. He often dreamed of a life of adventure, like Old Glass-Eyed Pete's, the Biglums' great-great-great-great-grandfather. Billy couldn't help loving sea tales, because the trunk that he slept in used to contain Old Glass-Eyed Pete's treasure. And the stories of his adventures still stirred inside like whispers. He'd sailed at least six of the seven seas, pirating chestfuls of doubloons, jewels and other booty. To a lonely skeleton boy trapped in a closet, no life looked so fair as a pirate's!

Billy imagined himself boarding a ship with his pirate crew. He'd swing from the highest yardarm, dagger grinding between his teeth, and land on the deck to claim the treasure for his fearsome crew. Then he'd wake with his sword arm thrust in the air, shouting, 'Plunder the treasure and scuttle the ship, boys!'

At first his parents were concerned about these bloodthirsty outbursts, but soon they put it down to an active imagination and acute boredom. Billy had asked about the swashbuckling figure in his dreams a number of times. His parents told him that Glass-Eyed Pete was the founder of the Biglum family and he had seen more strange lands and had more adventures than any three people they had ever met. But they seemed reluctant to say much more. Billy was sure there were dark secrets attached to the tales.

A small current of air wafted Billy's spiderweb curtains and he was reminded of the ratlines and shrouds on a tall ship. He climbed the nearest stack of trunks and cried, 'Into the rigging, me lads! And cast yer eyes for sails on the horizon.'

9

As Billy clattered up the trunks, Mr Bones lowered his paper. It crinkled like the frown on his forehead. 'Decette, I think it's time to give our boy some lessons in secret keeping.'

The comment caught Mrs Bones by surprise. She dropped her darning and blinked two luminous eyes. 'But young skeletons are supposed to receive sanctioned training at Miss Spinetip's School for Secret-Keeping Skeletons, and you know that's out of the question, considering Billy's situation.'

'Still and all, my dear, we can't have him caterwauling about forever, pretending he's a pirate. A bit of training will give him some purpose, I should think, even if we can't send him back to the Afterlife for schooling.'

'I suppose . . . well, he'll be quite excited when you tell him, there's no doubt about that.'

Billy, who hadn't listened to a word, scrambled around on top of the trunks a bit longer, harred a few more 'Har, maties!' and then thumped to the floor. He'd just spotted a glossy black beetle over by his sleeping trunk. It was Scamp, the closest thing he had to a friend. Billy had found him years before, scurrying under the floorboards.

Scamp enjoyed telling Billy the comings and goings in the rest of the house. He knew where the best piles of garbage were, where a comfortable sock had been left on the floor, and who had the loudest snores. Even these scraps of household intelligence captured Billy's interest.

Scamp's field report for today: more activity in the house than usual, mostly near the old playroom in the attic. Possibly someone new was visiting.

Indeed, someone was. The new arrival was Millicent Hues, but it would be some time before she and Billy met. And there was more to arrive, besides. Bound for the closet was a fresh shipment of secret trunks in need of careful storage. The close-knit Bones family was about to knit even closer.

CHAPTER 2

PRAIRIE STORM

Miss Hester Primly, the Biglums' housekeeper, had a face one would never describe as attractive. 'Wrinkled' and 'dry' were words that fitted nicely. At this particular moment, her eyes bulged with a mixture of shock and contempt, her eyebrows looked ready to fly off her face, and one nostril flicked in and out as all six feet of her bony figure glared down at a smashed teacup on the floor. Miss Primly swooped out of the parlour and into the grand hallway, leaving the Biglum ancestral portraits to stare in disgust.

In her high-collared black dress, she swished past rows of saluting armour and walls plastered high with Biglum portraiture. Apple-green ferns and potted palms were the only soft touches in the hardwood hall.

The house, for all its greatness, was never kept much brighter than the Boneses' closet—unless the Biglums were entertaining. Even outside on a sunny day, the manor cast a shadow of relentless pride that would have made the tallest man feel like a simpering shortcake. The house was a towering dedication to haughty airs.

Miss Primly moved past a score of maids polishing the floor. The smell of lemon deepened the crinkles in her nose. Each maid bent lower as the Primly storm gusted through to the end of the hallway and moved up the grand staircase. Most people would have needed a rest by then, but not Miss Primly. Sterner stuff, that's what she was made of, with some vinegar, cod liver oil and bitters thrown in for good measure.

Finally, Miss Primly slowed and entered the library.

The library was as grand as any other part of the manor. Leather-bound books packed shelves that raced to the ceiling, and a brass-railed walkway cut the height of the book stacks in two. Rolling ladders stretched from the floor to the walkway and from the walkway to the skylight, high above.

Busts of philosophers and literary notables circled the room, eyeing Miss Primly with suspicion. A grandfather clock chimed the quarter hour and the fireplace washed the room with dancing light.

Standing opposite the fireside, a man examined a pile of blueprints. He was squat as a barrel and looked mean as a mallet. The man, whose plump fingers drummed nervously, was Sir Barkley Braggety Biglum the Sixth, head of the house, lord of the manor, and general all-around big cheese.

Lost in thought, Sir Biglum stroked his coal-shovel jaw. His eyes skulked in the shadow of his bulky brow. Some men shared chummy nicknames like 'Monty' for 'Montgomery' or 'Algie' for 'Algernon'. But the warmest, chummiest name one could think of for Sir Barkley Braggety Biglum the Sixth was 'Sir'.

He was dressed informally in a cravat and smoking jacket. Smoke drifted up from his jacket and caressed his bald head, twisting off into the darkness. One could not be sure if the source of smoke was his cigar or his devilish heart.

A tiny 'ahem' from Miss Primly secured his attention.

'PRIMLY, what is it?' gruffed Sir Biglum. Because of his short stature, Sir Biglum had developed a habit of bouncing up on his toes to emphasize certain words. 'You know I HATE being disturbed when I'm working on my PLANS.'

She did know. He'd been labouring over these blueprints for months. Miss Primly went a full shade paler. Sir Biglum was the one person who gave her the shivers.

'It's a teacup, sir—' Miss Primly started.

'A teacup!' Sir Biglum cut her off. 'I should be interrupted from my BIGGEST plans to date . . . plans that will increase my fortune to the point where banks will join forces to build vaults big enough . . . just to hear about a TEACUP?' His eyes screwed into Miss Primly's.

She stepped half a heel click back. 'There's a bit more, sir. For weeks, objects have been out of place, even broken. This started after the arrival of your niece, Millicent. I thought I should inform you.'

'If she doesn't know how to behave herself PROPERLY,' said Sir Biglum, his eyelids low with

14

malice, 'see to it that she LEARNS . . . particularly before this year's ball. Her pitiful story will be FABULOUS for showcasing my generous nature.' He sniffed and then slammed his fists on the table. 'But you'd better be sure she doesn't EMBARRASS me, or I'll have you BOTH thrown out like gutter rats.' He grabbed his plans with a *smack* and turned his back.

Miss Primly glided out of the room. Oh, I'll take care of her, all right, she thought. I'll take care of her!

*   *   *

The flame in Sir Biglum's eyes cooled a few degrees. The girl had been a minor annoyance until now. In fact, he had forgotten that she had even come to stay at the manor.

Years rolled off Sir Biglum's face as he remembered his sister Julia. It had been a long time since he had had anything that you could call 'good' feelings. Greed was his constant companion now.

Yet he could almost feel a summer's breeze blowing from the memories of his childhood. He had spent so much time together with his brother and sister up in the playroom, since his father hadn't allowed the children to have friends. 'Riff-raff and ticky-tack children aren't for the likes of my fine family,' the Fifth would say.

Sir Biglum flushed as he remembered Julia leaving the manor years later, marrying Artemis Hues, a man far beneath the family. And it had been only days before the event of the century, the one the family scheduled every two years, the

15

bi-quadrennial Biglum Ball! *Just when the family was supposed to be at its most splendid. Her notable absence was an unforgivable embarrassment.* Her name was never mentioned in the household again.

An arranged marriage could have meant a welcome addition to the Biglum fortune. But running away to a life among the city's artists, musicians and intellectuals wouldn't put one penny into anyone's pocket. *Certainly not MINE!* (Sir Biglum often rose on his toes even when he was thinking.)

Then his headstrong sister had to go and get herself killed. *The potential for humiliation! It could have cost this family EVERYTHING!* Greed tickled the nape of Sir Biglum's neck. As he reached back to scratch, he remembered the drawings. He dismissed the past, settled back in the present, and considered his visions of the future.

CHAPTER 3

TWO GHOSTLY VISITORS

It's not every little girl who balances on tiptoes in the middle of a room and has her hair stroked by a floating hairbrush. If you were to stand quietly in a corner, you'd notice other peculiarities as well. Like a chest opening and closing of its own accord—different dresses hovering for a quick approval—or what appeared to be a three-way conversation with only one person present.

The little girl was Millicent, and judging by her smile, the goings-on were as welcome as carols at Christmas.

If you could then move from the corner and watch through Millicent's eyes, you'd see her parents, who had been killed in an accident. Their heads bent at an unnatural angle, to the right. When they stood next to one another, they seemed to be contemplating the same idea at the same time. Their amber hair and clothes billowed

17

slowly, as if they were underwater. (Local police had dredged them from the River Ire. Millicent's parents had been out in the country, painting on a boat. If she hadn't been staying with her best friend, Vanessa, they would have found all three Hueses floating that day, just five weeks before.) Now, her parents' touch was colder than a mackerel, and Millicent missed their warmth. But their translucent forms were filled with a beautiful gauzy light. Millicent was happy to have them around.

Her days had been long and lonely since her parents departed to the other side and she was always glad when they came back. 'Why can't you visit more often?' Millicent had asked them.

'Red tape, long queues at the railway stations and mutton-headed government officals,' was their reply. But when they *could* visit, Millicent updated them on the explores she'd made in the attic of the giant house, certain she'd been in rooms that people hadn't breathed in for generations.

What Millicent loved most was exploring and solving mysteries. What's behind that door? she would ask herself. What's in that box or under that hat?

So far, several hallway doors had defied Millicent's snooping. She had asked her parents if they could walk through the walls and open them from the other side. But just like parents anywhere, they told her those rooms were locked for a reason.

Soon she was in bed, arms wrapped tightly around her knees, watching her mother, Julia. She was hovering just above the bed, and Millicent was reminded of the golden tumble of perfume during nightly tuck-ins—in her old featherbed, in her old life.

Her father, Artemis, bobbing gently, fluffed her pillow. The cold fog of his ghost arm brushed by her, and she remembered when he was full of life and colour. He'd sit for hours over his canvases until his paintings glowed with beauty. When Millicent burst into his studio, he would stop, wipe his hands, and greet her like she'd just returned from a year-long sea cruise.

Millicent's parents had always made her feel special, and were still doing a fine job for two people nearly not there. Even now, in their translucent forms, they were generous with praise.

'Julia, my dear,' Millicent's father said, 'you're looking particularly lovely this evening—your glow is even more glow-y than last night. The Afterlife agrees with you.' Millicent's father always made the best of things, no matter which side of the grave.

'Artemis, if I could, you'd have me blushing,' her mother replied, reaching for his hand.

Love didn't appear to fade in the Afterlife.

'But look at how pretty Millicent is and how big she's getting.' Millicent was fully capable of blushing, and she did.

Millicent was someday going to be a 'looker', according to her father. Now she was a thin and wispy girl of eleven with rust-brown hair as independent as she was and a long nose that sometimes embarrassed her.

As for her room in the Biglum manor, it was empty as a poor man's pocket. It held only six items: a small bed, her trunk of clothing, a cracked washing bowl with an equally cracked pitcher, a bedside candle and a small box of matches.

The highlight of the room was a small window. It had no curtains, of course, but Millicent could look out on the lush countryside to the village of Houndstooth-on-Codswattle.

It was summer, and nature lounged gloriously beyond the manor's shadow. Millicent wanted to hike in the warm fields, raise her face, close her eyes and see the red glow of the sun through her eyelids; or maybe dip a few toes in the nearby river. But Miss Primly had been lurking too close each time Millicent tried to escape.

The thought of Miss Primly caused Millicent's lip to push out in a grump as her parents prepared to leave. Her mother was the first to see it, and tousled Millicent's hair.

She leaned forward, dissolving into mist, and whispered, 'You'll be all right.' And was gone.

Millicent struggled with sleep. She pulled the sheet to her face between balled-up fists and remembered her first meeting with Miss Primly. 'What an odious little girl,' were the housekeeper's first words. 'Understand this: you are to stay completely out of the way up in the attic. You are not to bother the staff in any way. And most certainly, you will never, ever disturb Sir Barkley Braggety Biglum the Sixth, because if you do, you little leech . . .' Miss Primly drew her index finger across her neck.

'I'm sure I should thank my uncle in person. It's the right thing to do,' Millicent said bravely. 'And what about schooling? My mother was helping me read the classics, and my father was teaching me music and art.'

Miss Primly's face twisted as she huffed a dry

laugh. 'Schooling? Here's your first lesson, and it's written on the back of my hand!'

She raised her hand to strike, but Millicent was too quick for her and was already on her way up to the attic.

Millicent had found her way up the endless stairs to the bleak room where she had slept since. Now she tossed a few more tosses, turned a few more turns, and missed her parents a bit more. She missed her best friend Vanessa too, and their secret trips to the roof to gaze at the city. Millicent even missed the musky fumes that drifted from the alleyways behind the old houses, and the constant clip-clopping and rumble of wagons.

Each memory drifted by, like a solemn funeral procession. Finally sleep was kind enough to shake loose a dream, and Millicent gratefully sank into slumber.

CHAPTER 4

MORE FAMILY SECRETS

Even though it was the deepest and deadest part of the night, a lively excitement was brewing in the closet. The Boneses were expecting Mr Cecil Benders, the weekly courier. This was the one night a week when Billy was allowed to stay up late, but tonight he was up later than usual. Mr Benders was taking his time.

Mr and Mrs Bones hunched over a trunk, carefully sorting the week's darkest secrets and tying the small packets in ruby red departmental ribbon for special storage.

Really nasty secrets are much too unpredictable to simply store in a trunk. They require delicate handling and a sturdy metal box. These particular secrets were quite hot. Mr Bones juggled them into the metal container and closed the lid.

Billy had often noticed a small brass box stored next to the larger ones. He had always wondered what was inside, but his parents would clam up at the slightest mention.

Mr and Mrs Bones were a gentlc pair, but they could hold fast to the thorniest of family secrets, especially their own. Billy was less practised and, truth be told, he could hold a secret no better than his stomach could hold a strawberry milkshake—which was not at all.

Mr Benders's weekly visit gave the family two great joys. One was the delivery of the *Eternal Bugle* (the Afterlife's leading newspaper) and the other was an excuse to have cocoa. Billy's family was crazy for the stuff. They would often say, 'Nothing warms the old bones like a good cup of hot chocolate,' and then clink their cups together.

Mrs Bones unpacked the kettle and eight cups and arranged them on a tray. Mr and Mrs Bones had spent hours teaching Billy the customs of cocoa drinking. He knew how to place one cup in his lap, just so, while drinking from the other (a necessity when one has no stomach). These days, he rarely spilled even one small drop. Mrs Bones filled a battered pot with chocolate, then set it on the metal box to catch the remaining heat.

Mr Bones spread a lace doily on a trunk and Mrs Bones set the tray on top. Just at that moment, the closet door creaked open and in limped a skeleton with a *hitchity-click*. This was Mr Benders. His normally good-natured face drooped with concern.

He adjusted the courier's bag slung over his shoulder. 'Master Billy, I need help with this load, if you've a mind to offer.'

Billy looked up. He was playing a game with Scamp. The little beetle liked to fetch dust balls.

He'd wiggle his antennae and squeak, 'Toss it again!'

Ignoring his tiny friend's pleas, Billy clambered to his feet and clicked across to the door. He was more than a little curious about Mr Benders's load. Three leather trunks were stamped with official Afterlife seals. Mr Benders muttered to himself and pushed one to the door with his foot for Billy to drag inside.

'Would love to use wishes to move these trunks around. 'Course that won't work on Earth.' Mr Benders groaned as he shoved the next trunk into the closet. 'I don't know what I was thinking, agreeing to take these along. The young lady ghost had the saddest tale, and the prettiest way of telling it. She had the Post and Packaging agent blubbering like a baby. I know I'll regret this someday soon—it's clear as the tears of Justice,' Mr Benders grumped, then pushed the last trunk towards Billy.

Billy knew that skeletons had a long association with the twin sisters Truth and Justice. Over the many years Mr Benders had made deliveries to the closet, he'd shared any number of dribs and drabs about the Afterlife. Billy had learned about the Department of Fibs and Fabrications, the section of the Afterlife government his parents worked for. He'd also heard a bit about the Investigative Branch and the Moral Authority, two of the departments run by ghosts—mean-spirited ones. Billy knew that the three departments didn't get along very well, and skeletons seemed to get the short end of the disagreements. The delivery of trunks from the Afterlife was definitely unusual. There were so many rules and regulations to

24

follow up there, Billy wasn't sure how the delivery had even been possible.

Mr Benders pressed his knuckles into his back. He dug around in his bag and pulled out a fresh newspaper and the usual small packet of departmental correspondence and handed them to Mr Bones. The old messenger nodded his respects, then abruptly turned to go.

Mrs Bones stopped her spoon in mid swirl. 'Won't you stay for some cocoa, Cecil?'

'Sorry, Decette, that load cost me too much time tonight. Besides, I'd rather put some distance between myself and those trunks. Suspect I ruffled a few Afterlife feathers by delivering them.' The old skeleton clacked out of the door.

'Too strange,' murmured Mrs Bones as she restacked the cups. 'And where on Earth are we to store them?'

Despite Mr Benders's warnings, Mr Bones looked pleased. He rubbed his hand bones together and smiled widely. 'A new shipment of secrets!'

Billy's mother rolled her eyes. 'The smell!' Secrets start to smell like old fish after they've been lying around in the dark for a while.

Billy had seen nothing like these trunks before. Lies and secrets would tumble in every so often, but they arrived in small packets. Mr and Mrs Bones would slide them into corresponding folders and store them in the appropriate trunk.

Secrets (especially dark ones) lead to lies. And one lie leads to another. Unchecked, they could twist, turn, and pile up until they become wild, wobbly constructions—so it was important to file them properly. Lars and Decette Bones had their work cut out for them separating little white lies from whoppers and teasing out truths from half-truths. All together, the lies and secrets the Biglums had built their history on would have dwarfed the manor itself.

The Boneses were always careful to keep the lies and secrets separate as they were quite different, lies being outright deceptions and secrets being hidden facts. However, both would explode in the light of truth.

When working in an official capacity, Mr Bones liked to wear his Department of Fibs and Fabrications cap. It looked like a train conductor's cap but with gold swirls embroidered into the flat top and a winged skull insignia at the front. He thought it looked dashing. Billy wasn't quite sure if Mrs Bones agreed, from the twinkle in her eye and sideways smile. The two Boneses worked side by side like a four-handed engine, stamping, filing and filling out the logbook.

There had been one or two times when Billy had nosed in too close. He'd read the documents and blurted out the secrets. Once voiced aloud, the secrets were no longer secret. A blinding globe of light would appear above the skeletons' heads and blast the secret with bright rays, causing the document to blow to bits. The globe was an Oculus: a glowing hole between this world and the Afterlife that conducts the light of truth.

Exposure to an Oculus is very painful. The heat from the explosion singed the skeletons each time. So Mr and Mrs Bones issued a new closet rule. *Rule 43: Billy must remain on the opposite side of the closet any time a trunk is open.*

Mr Bones whistled to himself (no small feat for

a skeleton) as he adjusted his cap. He pulled the first trunk forward and flipped open the latches. Mrs Bones looked at Billy, twirled her finger like she was stirring cocoa, then pointed to the back of the closet. Billy grudgingly turned his back and stepped away.

'Someday, I'll have my own secrets closet,' Billy whispered to Scamp.

The beetle's antennae flicked upright.

'Why should other skeletons have all the fun?' Billy continued.

Scamp reminded Billy of his other dreams by swashing a few sword strokes in the air.

Billy perked up. 'There are no rules against having a secrets closet on a pirate ship. I like that!'

While Billy and Scamp whispered, Mr Bones gaped into the trunk.

'Are you all right?' Mrs Bones asked, but Mr Bones didn't move. A rainbow glow from the trunk lit his bony face.

The glow caught Billy's eye. He docked his dreams of sailing ships.

'Hmm.' Mr Bones closed the lid and placed the next trunk before him. Again, a beautiful glow washed over his face as he opened it. 'Hm, hmm.'

Then Mr Bones, Mr Lars Bones, expert secrets keeper, official member of the Department of Fibs and Fabrications, custodian of half-truths and worse, did something remarkable. He revealed what was inside the trunk. 'Paintings.'

Mrs Bones and Billy hunched over and put fingers in their earholes, waiting for the explosion. But none came.

After a few seconds, Billy and Mrs Bones lowered their fingers and looked questioningly at

Mr Bones. 'Sorry to scare you,' he said, 'but they don't appear to be secrets.'

He set the second trunk aside and looked into the third. He flipped the paintings forward one by one, then paused. A sheet of carefully folded paper poked out between two frames.

Mr Bones removed it delicately, and dug absentmindedly in his jacket pocket for his spectacles. He put them on with a flick of his wrist and scanned the note. 'It's a letter from Artemis and Julia Hues. This is most unusual, but I can't find even the smallest lie here. I'll read it to you.'

Secrets Closet
High Manners Manor

Dear Mr and Mrs Bones,
My name is Artemis Hues and my wife is Julia. Please accept our apology for the imposition of our three trunks. They are family business, however. Julia, as you may remember from a flurry of documents about fourteen years ago, is the sister of Sir Barkley Braggety Biglum VI. We ran off and married without the family's blessing.

We had a wonderful married life, but we are now dead, and imagine that we will remain so for a long time. We've managed to persuade a kindly messenger to send these trunks along to you. He went well beyond the call of duty (and perhaps bent a few Afterlife rules in the process).

The trunks contain my most important works of art. As Monsieur Henri Bouche De Sourire, a gallery owner, happily told me shortly before I crossed to the Afterlife, they are worth a fortune.

That brings me to the final point: our daughter,

Millicent, whom Sir Biglum has recently taken in. We wish the paintings to become Millicent's when she is old enough. And we would most assuredly NOT like to see them sold off to increase the fortunes of Sir Biglum.

Julia and I beg with all our ghostly hearts, please keep them safe for Millicent. Thank you,

Artemis and Julia Hues

Mr Boncs removed his spectacles. Billy was pleased to be let in on some of the happenings in the rest of the house.

He didn't see the worry in his father's eyes, but Mrs Bones did. 'These trunks are most irregular, Lars. It nettles me that Mr Benders even brought them. Perhaps we should ask him to take them back.'

Mr Bones chewed on his pipe and frowned. 'No . . . no . . . I don't care how irregular. The Hueses are family members and protection is due to them if requested.' He examined the letter again. 'They've asked that the paintings remain secret from Sir Biglum. And yet, they shouldn't be secret from Millicent. Quite a puzzle.' Mr Bones tapped his chin with his pipe stem. 'It seems to me that we need to issue a claims form.'

Mr Bones grabbed an official form and penned in the details. Mrs Bones filed it in a battered walnut filing cabinet. After that, Mrs Bones reluctantly directed Mr Bones in rearranging the trunks. When he and Mrs Bones had finished, he checked the pocket watch he wore suspended on a gold chain off his herringbone jacket pocket. The watch accented his movements with a hypnotic swaying motion.

Closing the lid of his watch with a click of his bony thumb, he announced, 'Billy, hop into your trunk, it's bedtime.'

'Don't forget to dust off first,' Mrs Bones reminded. 'I'll be there in a moment to tuck you in.'

Mrs Bones had always thanked her stars that they'd been allowed to bring a few possessions to their posting on Earth: like her cups and saucers, small writing desk and spindly chairs. But it was the nightgowns, bedclothes and horse blankets that really helped make the small closet more cosy.

Billy pulled one of Mr Bones's old nightshirts over his head and slipped into his trunk. It was a while before he was able to dismiss the excitement of sharing a family secret. Mrs Bones's soft singing and her ivory smooth caresses finally moved him into sleep's gentle embrace.

After Billy sawed off a few child-sized snores, Mrs Bones sat down next to her husband with a look of concern. 'What's been eating at you, dumpling?'

Mr Bones removed the smokeless pipe from his teeth and dropped his study of the ceiling. 'Sorry, Decette. I feel a bit weighed down by secrets, is all . . .'

A scratching sound scrabbled from the corner by the boxes. The brass one knocked about as if a small animal was trapped inside.

'Oh, those secrets . . .' said Mrs Bones. She settled wearily next to her husband. Neatly stacked memories stirred where her heart would have been.

'So many secrets . . . It's a lonely burden we

skeletons carry from day to day. Not made any lighter by the secrets of our own,' Mr Bones sighed.

'Perhaps it's time we tell him.' Mrs Bones took her husband's hand. 'He has every right to know.'

'It grinds my teeth to let any secret go, but it's true, my dear. He has every right. Perhaps at the proper time.'

Mr Bones patted his wife's white hand as they watched Billy sleep. They sat quietly arm in arm, wrapped in parental concern, until it was time for bed.

*   *   *

In the solitary hours just past midnight, the manor groaned softly, trapped in its own hard-hearted slumber. All else was quiet save for a curious visitor listening on the other side of the keyhole.

CHAPTER 5

THE OTHER SIDE

A papyrus calling card stamped with a gold-leafed 'G' burst from a ball of light and floated into the darkening room. Magical sparks faded with the light.

It was evening at the temple of Maat, the winged goddess of truth and justice.

Fifty oiled and muscled servants carried torches into the throne room, where tall pillars rose well above the torchlight's reach while Maat loomed from her perch on a massive stone block wall. More servants surrounded the throne, fanning and peeling grapes for the seated high priestess, Miss Cornelia Chippendale.

This plump high priestess had obviously not been chosen for her beauty. Her black Cleopatra wig was askew and she would have looked better in wool, patrolling the stacks in a library. A pair of reading spectacles was perched on her nose and she hummed quietly to herself as she read the note scratched on the back of the card.

Miss Cornelia Chippendale was chief assistant to Commissioner Pickerel of the Investigative Branch. 'What's this? Skeletons taking liberties with secrets procedures . . . improper storage of inappropriate material . . . just what the commissioner's been looking for!'

She heaved herself out of the throne and huffed across the temple room and into an official-looking hallway. The marble floors and walls of the echoey hallway appeared to go on forever (and probably did). Statues of ex-administrators and department heads lined up proudly on both sides. There had been many over the millennia. After all, a term of service lasts three hundred years.

All manner of beings bustled along on Afterlife business. Skeletons with armfuls of files kept to themselves. Wraiths in pairs carried on lively conversations. They passed right through other ghosts, equally deep in conversation. A number of bodies in various stages of decay were not as quick on their feet and other Afterlifers stacked up behind them, waiting to pass. These poor creatures would one day become skeletons, but the process of dropping bits and pieces of body takes years. Most of the hallway's occupants were normal ghosts like Miss Chippendale. They looked very much as they did on Earth, except for their transparency and glow.

Much, much farther down the hall was the darker portion of the Afterlife, with its imps, demons and all kinds of evils. The Afterlife government is divided into the side that relishes corruption and the side that exposes it. A war between the two has ripped apart the Afterlife for as long as there has been light and darkness— which is a very long time.

Miss Chippendale stopped in front of a door marked *Commissioner Pickerel*, knocked and walked in. The frumpy priestess found herself standing on a cloud with other fleecy clouds and blueness stretching to the horizon. A hand-carved mahogany desk sank down in the main cloud's spongy floor. Behind the desk sat a middle-aged gentleman. He was scrubbed to a glossy sheen, tall, and thin as a javelin. Every detail, from his combed grey hair to his polished shoes, was in perfect order. Sharpest of all was the steel-tipped stare of his cold grey eyes.

'Now, Miss Chippendale, what may I do for you?' Pickerel asked.

'Well, sir, *this* just came in, and I thought you might want to have a look at it.' She politely blinked the card into an official piece of departmental stationery and handed it to the commissioner. As he read, his expression darkened.

'These skeletons. Have they no shame?' The commissioner glared at Miss Chippendale. 'And who, in thundering blue skies, delivered those trunks, and how did they get official Post and Packaging seals?'

'That's a bit of a mystery, sir. My source showed up only after the trunks had arrived.'

The commissioner leaned over his desk. It sank several more centimetres into the cloud floor. 'This will not do! We'll get to the bottom of this, or half the department's off to Nevermore!'

Miss Chippendale grimaced. Nevermore, the

Light Side's darkest hole, was Pickerel's favourite place to send misfits.

'We do know who sent the boxes, though. See right there? Artemis and Julia Hues.' She pointed to the document hopefully.

'I'm more concerned that the trunks went through our own Post and Packaging Department. I want to know who's been rubbing elbows with skeletons.' The commissioner's brows tangled into a frown. 'Working with skeletons! They're far beneath us, with all their earthly business. Every ghost in the Afterlife knows that!'

Miss Chippendale shared many of the commissioner's feelings about skeletons. Pickerel had stated on many occasions that skeletons didn't belong in government service, let alone hold power over two departments. 'Give them the run of Earth, and leave them there!' he often said.

One of Pickerel's cold eyes quivered as he considered the document again. 'This couple . . . Artemis and Julia Hues. Get me their files.'

Miss Chippendale pulled on a long velvet cord and a large cloudbank parted, revealing a skyscraper-sized filing cabinet. Cherubs buzzed up and down the immense object. Miss Chippendale requested the file from a wraith sitting behind a hovering desk, who bellowed the order through a megaphone. Seconds later, Miss Chippendale handed the file to her impatient boss.

He sifted through it for a moment and then looked up. 'Right.' He closed the file with a thump. 'No more travels Earthside for them any time soon. And if they try anything else out of the ordinary, we'll ship them off to Nevermore.'

He returned his attention to the departmental

stationery. 'As for those skeletons, recall them to the Afterlife immediately!'

'Pardon me, Commissioner, but that might be overstepping your authority. Oversecretary Underhill and his two departments are in charge on the other side.'

'Blast and bother! Underhill's the most underhand skeleton of the lot! The law's been broken!'

'But sir, they do have rights.'

'Forget their rights! Break the law and there go your rights!'

'You might want to clear that with the Moral Authority first, don't you think?'

Commissioner Pickerel rubbed his long chin. 'Perhaps, Miss Chippendale. But I tell you what. Let's gather as much information as we can first. This might be just the thing to chuck the oversecretary and the rest of his skeletons right out of the Afterlife. We could end up with two more departments under our control! For the good of the Afterlife, of course.' Pickerel examined his perfectly clean nails as Miss Chippendale nodded.

'Of course, sir. For the good of the Afterlife.'

'It's a stroke of luck that we have an informant on that side. I must say, Chippendale, good job.' He tossed her the file.

She passed it off to the filing cherubs and was soon back in her torchlit office conjuring up peeled grapes and a few more muscular servants.

CHAPTER 6

HALLWAY GOSSIPS

Martha bustled into Millicent's room with a pitcher of fresh water. 'Morning, ducks!'

The plump maid sloshed over to Millicent's trunk and splashed water into the bowl, then began dusting. 'I'd be up and dressed if I were you, dearie,' she said. 'Miss Primly's due up any time now.'

Martha was the uppermost upstairs maid, responsible for the fifth floor and attic. It was, without a doubt, the easiest duty in the household, because as far as Millicent knew, she and Martha were the only ones to ever come up to the top floors. Martha was an odd fit in the manor. She was filled with more good nature than her body could hold, and it spilled from her constantly as she bounced through her day.

'Into one of your dresses now, dearie. Miss Primly's coming and I've business to attend to.

Ooh, looks like you've already laid one out for yourself. It will be nice to see you out of these dreadful black mourning dresses. I bet you can't wait.'

Millicent was soon washed, dressed and hair brushed, Martha chattering all along the way. After Martha left, her one-way conversation continued down the hallway.

Just when the attic had returned to its normal solitude, *snick-snack, snick-snack*—Miss Primly's hard heels made their way up to the attic. Millicent busied herself as best she could.

*   *   *

Ninnies and nincompoops, Miss Primly huffed, *this is a long way up.* She hadn't made the trip to the attic for a number of years, but with the little troublemaker up there, one could only guess how many trips she'd have to make.

When she entered the room, Millicent's back greeted her. The girl was making her simple bed. Hester Primly didn't, as a rule, single out any particular person or thing for hating—she was equal opportunity—but there was something about this girl that whipped up the rage in her heart. *Chaos. The girl reeks of it. Just look at that hair, higgledy-piggledy, going this way and that.*

Primly's patience could neither wear thin, nor wear fat, because she had none to begin with. So it was with distinct impatience that she snapped, 'Millicent!'

Millicent jumped and turned. There was a good deal more than fear reflected in her face. A pinch of pouting, a teaspoon of temper, and a helping of

38

heroism hid there too. *Most unusual,* Miss Primly mused. *But I'll have the arrogance squeezed out of her soon.*

'I distinctly remember telling you that you are to stay up here in the attic, unless—and only unless—you are in the kitchen having your meals. Isn't that so?' she screeched.

Millicent nodded slowly.

'What do you have to say about the teacup, then?'

Millicent looked blank.

'Come now. You're not going to deny it?' Miss Primly looked like a crow inspecting a corncob, head turned and favouring one eye.

'Sorry, I'm—'

'Sorry isn't going to fix a smashed teacup, is it? Sorry isn't fit for filling at the Biglum family's next high tea.' Miss Primly turned both flaming eyes on her now.

'I . . .' Millicent began again.

'Don't interrupt me, you little boil! Didn't that mother of yours teach you anything? If she did, it's a pathetic job she made of it. You'll be washing dishes downstairs in the scullery for the next two nights as punishment. And if I hear another word out of you, we'll make a month of it!'

Millicent's face burned and tears glistened in her eyes. But Miss Primly's lit up in a nasty smile. *Best entertainment I've had all day.* She left the room, calling back over her shoulder, 'Cook will expect you at ten o'clock sharp tonight!'

*　　　*　　　*

After the last echoes of Miss Primly's footsteps

retreated, Millicent gathered herself together and declared that she wasn't going to let the old prune get the better of her. She splashed the evidence of tears into the water-filled bowl.

Out of the window, the morning was slipping into a lovely summer's day. Millicent absorbed the luscious landscape colours the way a diver fills his lungs before submerging, as she prepared to face the gloomy household. Morning was one of the few times of day she was allowed to get something to eat in the kitchen.

Suddenly, Millicent stiffened. Somewhere in a very unused room in the back of her mind, past memories of birthdays and hugs, walks in the parks and dancing kites in the sky, down an unused corridor, a voice whispered a warning: 'Someone is watching you.'

The back of her neck tingled. Through the half-open door, Millicent saw a scarlet streak disappear down the stairwell, followed by a sniggering laugh. A swampy smell trailed behind.

Millicent scampered in pursuit. It was everything she could do to keep her heels from banging on every step. She hit the next floor running on tiptoes. Tittering came from the floor's main hallway. She was about to dash out of the servants' back hall when she saw four housemaids going about their chores. The red shape *whooshed* around the corner at the far end of the hall.

Millicent pressed against the wall and peered around the corner.

The housemaids were rolling up rugs and polishing floors. They whispered as they worked, afraid that Miss Primly might catch them. Each of them had suffered at the hard hand of Primly.

The oldest and chubbiest popped up on her knees, 'Bless my bloomers, this house has the coldest breezes. Anyone else feel it?'

'That overheated imagination of yours ought to warm you right up, Lucy. You always have the silliest stories,' the youngest one quipped. The others snorted in their sleeves.

As the maids continued in snickering whispers, the red shape peeked back into the hallway. Under its flowing scarlet hood and cloak, the apparition looked snakelike. It slithered through the air towards the whispering maids, two eyes floating in the centre of the hood's dark opening. As it drifted closer, its eyes rotated away, revealing a large ear.

Air drew into the apparition like a backward whistling wind. The more the cloaked creature overheard, the larger it swelled. Soon it wriggled and danced like a balloon in a breeze.

The apparition smiled serenely as its snake tongue flickered at the corner of its lips. The slithering shape was Gossip. While most manifestations preferred to cosy up inside one person's heart, this one preferred to flit from person to person, binding hearts together in a hateful web of half-truths. It's hard to say who first invited the manifestation into the manor, but now that it was tangled in so many hearts, it would be nearly impossible to remove.

The manifestation swam back and forth over the maids, whispering things that Millicent, straining as she might, couldn't overhear. After expelling nearly half its girth, it skulked away. But Gossip's belch of hideous red gas remained to colour the maids' conversation.

The plump maid suddenly switched subjects. 'I

hear tell the young niece upstairs is batty as a bell tower.'

'Go on with you, Lucy, where'd you get that?'

'It's what they say, Daphne. She speaks to those who aren't there.'

'Ohhhh, we've heard that tale more than once in these old halls. Could be idle chitchat . . . But where there's smoke, there's usually fire.'

'Aye, that's what I say.'

'She gives me the walloping willies when I see her traipsing down to the kitchen. Cracked, she is.'

'Like an old bowl.'

'Like a teacup in a monkey house.'

'Crackers she is and crackers she'll stay. Gets it from that mother of hers. Talk about being a penny short of a pound! She went running off to marry a man who hasn't even got two coins to jingle in his pocket.'

Millicent walked solemnly back to the servants' stairwell. She had lost her appetite, even though her stomach had been grumbling for food minutes before. Millicent decided to return to her room.

She climbed the long staircase, missing her parents more with every step. At the top, she leaned heavily against the handrail. Her usual path was straight ahead to her room, but she noticed a few crumbs on the bare wooden floor. They led away in the opposite direction to a door that was usually locked. It stood ajar.

CHAPTER 7

A REPORT FROM THE FIELD

Billy sat transfixed. His body was still but his mind was running, jumping and kicking in the air. He imagined himself inside each one of the remarkable paintings. Now he was visiting a salty harbour, bathed in sea greens and deep summer blues. Billy could see the waves slapping and the grand dame ships rising higher on the tide. As his imaginary self clattered on an ancient wooden pier, he was sure he heard the cries of seagulls.

The tiny sounds continued until Billy realized it was Scamp. The beetle had a report from the field. Billy reluctantly put the canvas back in the chest. Mrs Bones looked up as she heard Billy close the trunk's lid, *ka-thunk*. She was doing her best to mend Billy's socks while Mr Bones hid behind his newspaper, sneaking an afternoon snooze.

Scamp cleared his throat with a high-pitched *harrumph*. He stood before Billy like he was ready

43

to address the House of Lords. Billy leaned forward, facing his friend. He had worked hard to learn 'Bug' since he'd first met his insect friend. With little else to do besides dream of pirating and clamber on chests, he had welcomed the distraction. Billy would have been the first to admit he understood the language far better than he spoke it. But he used his bony fingers quite well as antennae, even though some of the higher chirps were too difficult. This didn't strain the friendship much, because Scamp was fonder of talking than listening.

The teeny black beetle stood on his hind legs, dusted himself off, and began his report.

There had been some kind of accident in the kitchen. Scamp had been looking for scraps of food under the loose floorboards when a great river of beef gravy had carried him away. He enjoyed the tasty ride right up to the point where the gravy river tipped over the edge of the subfloor, and he shot down into a yawning wall gap.

He fell, past basement, past sub-basement, through to sub-sub-basement, then slammed into a pool of gravy on a hard rock floor. The next thing he remembered was drifting though a crack in the wall that brought him into another part of the house, an area he had never been in before. The dungeon-like room was carved out of a twisted cave. It was empty, except for rusty chains on the walls covered by cobwebs and a dusty trunk in the middle of the floor.

Scamp thought that the trunk looked a lot like the sea chest Billy slept in.

'Another sea chest! Bouncing barnacles!' gasped

Billy. Scamp jumped at the interruption, and his antennae quivered. He tossed Billy a tiny frown and continued.

After Scamp had indulged in a few slurps of the gravy and a delicious burp, he inspected the trunk. He scampered up the side and heard a voice echoing inside.

It had sounded very pirate-like, and Scamp thought that Billy would be interested.

As he finished his report, Scamp snapped off a little salute. 'Wonders and williwaw!' Billy cried. 'There are some remarkable things going on around here these days!'

CHAPTER 8

A FRIEND IN NEED

Crumbs? Millicent thought. *Where did they come from?* Martha was the likely source, being the only other person who regularly came up into the attic. But one could never be certain in this crazy house.

A bold explorer like Millicent lives to find out where trails of breadcrumbs lead, and what's behind newly unlocked doors. Millicent skipped down the hall, the misery of the morning forgotten. She passed a lonely old grandfather clock, then pressed her hand to the door that stood ajar. It creaked obligingly and she stepped into another dim hallway. A long row of doors lined either side. The smell of cedar wood was everywhere.

A few of the doors were unlocked, so naturally Millicent had to take a look. She poked her head into dark rooms where she could barely make out the dusty wooden boxes and furniture jammed inside. These rooms were even rougher than the rest of the top floor. The walls were made from slats of unfinished pine with plaster plumped out from between each thin wooden strip.

Thumps, bumps and creaks were common in the old house, and in this gloom she felt an especially nasty chill. At the end of the hallway, faint light cracked under a door.

Millicent turned the door's porcelain knob and found herself in a children's playroom. The circular room had at least some sign of decoration. Faded hand-painted wall-paper graced the walls. A section had curled away from the plaster, bowing politely to the three windows in the room. There were pictures of storybook fairies and elves frozen in discoloured paint over the yellowing paper.

Sun-bleached and frayed sheer curtains moved softly by the opened windows that matched the wall's curve. An expert's hand must have crafted the moulding, sills and glass. Clearly more care and money had gone into this room than other less public parts of the house. The care had lessened over the years. But the room was surprisingly dust-free.

Three-quarters of the circular room was taken up by the playroom, and the other quarter was boxed off by an adjoining room. Its door was closed.

A chestnut brown rocking horse with a bedraggled mane stood guard in front of the toys and books neatly lined up in low shelves around the edge of the room. The horse's back rose nearly to Millicent's shoulders. It looked like it would offer a splendid ride.

A toy sailing boat leaned dry-docked in a stand,

its sail hung heavily with disuse. Several china dolls with ring-curled brown hair and old-fashioned ruby and green velvet dresses sat on the shelf below. Once-fluffy petticoats sagged in their laps, and a few of the dress seams were split, but their painted faces were still bright. One of them looked like the twin of an old doll Millicent's mother had kept since childhood. She'd often let Millicent brush its hair, gently. That doll was at least as old as the ones here.

'The dolls haven't had much love for a long time,' an old voice spoke up behind her.

Millicent almost leaped out of her skin. She turned quickly and faced an oddly familiar white-haired woman.

'Would you like to play? Go ahead, pick one up.' The old woman looked at Millicent, and a hint of concern clouded her face. 'Or perhaps you're hungry? Would you like to have some finger sandwiches, dear? Martha's just been by with a tray.'

The old lady tapped her cane on the floor twice, cleared her throat, then shuffled into the other room. Her cane ticked off a downbeat on every other step.

Once Millicent felt securely back in her skin, she realized just how hungry she was. She followed the old woman into the other room.

The room was luxurious compared to Millicent's. Two more windows let in soft light. The walls were ivory, and a rust-coloured oriental rug warmed the worn wood floor. The white-haired woman hung her cane from one arm, then teetered a silver tray to a lace-covered tea table. It held several delicate crustless sandwiches and a

48

tiny wrapped chocolate surrounded by crumpled foil.

The old lady looked at the lone chocolate and blushed. 'Sorry to say, it's the last of the bonbons. I'm afraid I have a weakness for the stuff.'

But Millicent's eye was on a cucumber sandwich. She grabbed it quickly, and swallowed almost without chewing.

She looked at the old lady, hoping for more, and was met by an encouraging smile. In a few blinks, the rest were gone. 'My goodness, dear, you *are* hungry. Let's have some more sent up, shall we? And perhaps more chocolate.'

Next to the door was a velvet-covered tube with a brass cap that extended down through the floor. The old woman unhooked it from its holder, removed the cap, and blew into the tube.

Millicent heard a tinny voice answer. The old lady shouted back, 'Ahoy! Please bring me another setting for lunch, straight away. I'm entertaining. Thank you.'

She popped the brass cap back on and motioned for Millicent to sit in one of two wingback chairs next to the table and the remains of lunch.

'She'll be back by and by.' She sat down opposite Millicent, leaning her cane on the couch. Embossed at the base of the cane's silver handle was the Biglum crest.

The room was tastefully furnished. The four-poster bed was near one window, its faded curtains closed. Three children's portraits were lined up on a dressing table, each one no bigger than a child's palm. The dressing table's mirror was covered in black cloth. A black ribbon draped across two of the pictures. Near the other window stood a spindle-legged writing desk and chair.

The old woman had kind eyes that drifted from absentmindedness to shocking concentration. Her face was a bit doughy, but beautiful. She wore a high-necked buttoned dress with a brooch on the collar. Her dress was black as grief, just like Millicent's. There was a portrait painted on the brooch, and Millicent examined it closely. She blinked, then blinked again. The portrait looked just like her, except for the hair. The hair was long and soft, like her mother's.

'I don't suppose we should forget our manners, my dear. Perhaps we should introduce ourselves,' suggested the old woman. 'My name is Dame Madeleine Biglum and I would swear to His Majesty the King himself, you look just like my late daughter Julia.'

'That was my mother's name,' Millicent replied. 'My name is Millicent.'

Dame Madeleine Biglum stared at Millicent for a while, eyes wider than an open-handed invitation. 'Perhaps I should reintroduce myself, then. I am your grandmother. Grandmother Maddy, if you'd like. Maddy is what my favourite people call me, and I hope I'm not being presumptuous in wishing that you would be one of those in the very near future.'

Millicent stared back, her eyes eating up the old woman as happily as she'd been eating cucumber sandwiches just moments before.

The old woman extended an unsteady hand and stroked Millicent's cheek. Her touch felt like antique paper, the crinkles made soft by age. It was so much warmer than a ghost's caress.

'And now, my dear,' Dame Biglum said with

50

misting eyes, 'tell me how it is you've come to be here.'

Millicent sank into her chair, wrapping her arms tight to her chest, and withdrew into tear-stained memories. They were memories she would rather not disturb, but her grandmother's question had roused them.

She remembered black cloth. The signs of mourning were draped over mirrors and pictures throughout her family's loft. Her friend Vanessa's mother had tried to help, but she was a widow with her own family's welfare to worry about. She couldn't spare much more than a few cold meals and a look-in on Millicent from time to time. Vanessa too was busy with lessons and housework. Vanessa's mother did arrange a funeral, though. She didn't have much money, so the minister rushed through the reading.

The artist's loft where Millicent grew up was the top floor of an aged apartment building. It leaned shoulder to shoulder among other working-class buildings like friends sharing secrets. The loft, which had always been bright with flowers and rich cooking smells, had turned grey and dingy almost overnight.

Sad days followed, yet Millicent also felt hopeful. She was sure her parents were going to come back, laughing and smelling fresh and wonderful. They'd sweep her up in their arms and all would be well. But grief and loneliness were her only visitors.

The passing days had been painful. But eventually, to Millicent's joy and relief, her parents returned in their ghostly forms. They had calmed her crying at night and helped her write a letter to her uncle, Sir Biglum. She had heard them mention him a few times in passing, usually when they were pointing out a particularly conceited person walking by.

Only a week after sending her letter, she had found herself on a train heading north, towards High Manners Manor.

A great show was made of collecting Millicent. This was the public side of Sir Biglum. Privately, he could not have cared less about her. *Get the little pest here as soon as possible, but make a display of it,* were his secret instructions. His lawyers, Messrs Hack, Whack and Plunder, were happy to oblige. Millicent was whisked to the local train station in an open carriage faster than lickety-split. The lawyers arranged for newspaper photographers and a brass band playing 'Come Back My Darling to Your Old Family Home' to show Uncle Biglum's tender concern.

Soon enough, the lawyers dropped Millicent at the massive mahogany doors of High Manners Manor, then slunk back to their carriage.

Millicent's sigh sounded lonely as an old teddy bear stuffed into storage. Dame Biglum inched forward. 'Are you well, dear? Would you rather not talk about it?'

Millicent shook off the memories and looked into her grandmother's milky blue eyes. They squinted with worry. Taking a deep breath, she told her sad tale as best she could. She left out the part about her ghostly parents, unsure how a grown-up would react.

Partway through, Martha arrived with a new tray of cucumber sandwiches, lemon tea with honey and more chocolates. Millicent looked nervously at Martha for fear that she'd snitch to Miss Primly. But Dame Biglum was quick with assurances that Martha knew how to keep matters under her cap. Martha nodded a sympathetic agreement.

Millicent continued, and tears gathered in Dame Biglum's eyes. When Millicent finished, her grandmother's shoulders slumped. The room turned colder.

'Oh, it's you again,' Dame Biglum said as she turned towards the darkened window. 'Well, you might as well have a seat, seeing how long your usual stays are.'

'Oh the poor dotty thing, she's at it again,' Martha whispered to Millicent. 'Seems like she's always talking to thin air. That's why Sir Biglum shut her away up here in the first place.'

But Millicent and Dame Biglum were sharing a vision that Martha couldn't see.

A shadow sat on the windowsill where only emptiness had been before. Other shadows stretched from under the bed, around candlesticks and behind picture frames. Creeping across the walls they came, and merged into the seated shadow.

The shade rose from its chair and glided towards Millicent. Two glossy eyes floated in its sunken face, staring at her chest like it was the lid to her soul.

Millicent was afraid her heart would stop. She reached for her grandmother and slid out of her chair.

'No!' groaned Dame Biglum. 'I'll *not* lose another child to this house! I've banished you once and I'll do it again.' Dame Biglum slammed her cane on the floor and struggled to her feet.

The shade looked nearly as shocked as Martha. It swirled like black ink dropped into a glass of water. The maid reached her mistress in several heavy steps. But the shade twisted into a cloud that thinned and disappeared.

'Are you all right, Madam? Had one of your spells?'

Before answering, Dame Biglum pressed her hands over Millicent's. She whispered in a voice that reminded Millicent of a soothing cello, 'Don't worry, we'll talk of this later, my dear.' Then she turned to Martha. 'It most certainly would have been one of my spells, if not for our young visitor.'

'I'll clear up this clutter then, Madam.' Millicent automatically rose to stack plates too. Dame Biglum looked at her granddaughter curiously, then shrugged and pitched in as well.

'I hope you don't mind my saying, Madam, but Cook's not going be pleased that she had to make a lunch for Miss Millicent. Could get her into a bit of a scrape.' Martha scratched the side of her nose and then scooped up the tray.

Dame Biglum glanced at Millicent before replying, 'If you would be so kind as to inform Cook that it was one of my *unusual* visitors whom I was entertaining and not mention Millicent . . .'

Martha nodded and smiled, then trundled the tray back down to the kitchen.

*   *   *

'Millicent, I see you have the unenviable talent of being able to see things which ought not to be there.' Her grandmother's voice was touched with sadness.

Millicent nodded. 'They seem to be everywhere you look in this house. What are they?'

Dame Biglum looked wistfully out of the window for a moment and then said, 'I have it on the authority of a once close friend that they are manifestations. Despicable creatures. That one, Despair, feasted on my heart more than once. Most recently when I heard of your mother's passing away. It was everything I could do to cast the dreadful thing off.'

Dame Biglum put her hand to her thin lips and grew quiet.

'I saw a different one earlier.' Millicent shuddered.

Dame Biglum dropped her hand and sat straighter.

'You must be ever so careful around them. Never let them into your heart, no matter how they try to seduce you. They will suck the Goods straight out of you.'

'The Goods?'

'Why yes, my dear. For every one of the Bads there is also a Good.' Dame Biglum lifted her cane and said, 'As bumpy a ride as life is, it's balanced. Cowardice is matched by Bravery, Gossip by Discretion, Despair by Hope, and so on.'

'Why haven't I seen Bravery hanging about?'

'I'm sure you have a healthy supply of Bravery. But you carry the Goods in your heart. We all arrive on this earth with them tucked away safely. Sadly, some people choose to befriend the Bads, and soon all that's left of their hearts are shells of darkness.'

Millicent chewed her bottom lip. 'Who was the

friend that told you about this?'

'He was a friend who helped me many times in this mournful manor. And he knows, because he wasn't of this earth. He was a ghost. But he stopped visiting a long time ago, sadly, at a time I could have used him most.'

Dame Biglum leaned forward again. 'Let's not talk of such things now. It's better to concentrate on the living.'

'You're right,' Millicent agreed bravely. 'As horrible as those creatures are, I think Miss Primly is worse.'

Dame Biglum went pale. 'I'm terribly sorry, Millicent, but there are two people in this household whom I refuse to discuss. One is the *woman* that you just mentioned,' she spat out the word *woman*. 'The other is the present master of this household.'

'You mean Sir Big . . .'

'Millicent,' Dame Biglum cut her off, 'I won't have you mentioning his name again or I'll be having more unwanted visitors in here and worse than the one you've just seen. I'm an old woman, my dear, and I'm tired.' She checked the window to make sure nothing was there. 'I'm afraid this has all been a bit much for me. I would really love it if you'd come back for a visit tomorrow. You've done me so much good, but I need a rest now. There's a dear girl, give me a hug before you go.'

Millicent embraced her grandmother, then paused at the door. 'Can I borrow a doll and maybe a book?'

'Oh, yes! They need the company as much as you. Just one thing before you go. Stay up in the attic and out of the way as much as possible. It's ever so much safer.'

Millicent closed the door and picked a doll with amber curls, a green velveteen dress, and matching green eyes that opened and closed. Then she found a book, *The Secret Sleuths of Wimpole Hall*. It was about a shadowy society of toddlers who use brilliant logic and an endless supply of luck to uncover one mystery after the next.

The doll seemed to blink in wide-eyed wonder as Millicent showed her the book. She named the doll Helen. Such a sunny name, perfect for filling her dreary room.

Millicent spent a good portion of the day back in her room with her new playmate, reading stories of budding detectives on dangerous missions. She paused every so often to tell Helen how a proper sleuth, like herself, would have avoided such and such a jam. Occasionally she caressed her doll's cheek as she recalled her grandmother's touch.

CHAPTER 9

UNCLE GRIM

Mr Bones loved reading his paper. It was the closest he could get to the Afterlife from his closet on Earth. He scanned every word, digging for the smallest morsels and savouring each scrap of Afterlife news.

Rustling his paper, he winked at his wife, and clamped a self-assured smile around his pipe stem—until he heard horse hooves clomping outside.

'It's Uncle Grim!' shrieked Billy. Now this was a rare treat indeed! He would have recognized the sound of his uncle's midnight stallion anywhere. The horse's name was Phlegyas, but Uncle Grim had let Billy nickname him Fleggs.

The horse was a mighty beast but was not solid like his skeleton rider. He was more force than horse: a collection of dark sparks and glowing stars. Most living creatures couldn't see him until their time on Earth was up.

A low voice rumbled in the hallway, and then the door was flung open. Uncle Grim stood wrapped in his unearthly shroud of doom. But before Grim could sweep his cloak off, Billy jumped into his arms. Fleggs eyed the skeletons curiously from out in the hallway.

'Ah Billy, you're a spark in a heart that's grown too cold. It's good to see you, lad—you too, Decette. And even you, baby brother.' He removed his cloak and then playfully jabbed his brother's shoulder. Grim's black uniform was cut like a cavalry officer's, with double-breasted buttons and braid-trimmed shoulders. His leather gloves were almost as glossy as his riding boots.

Mr Bones glared at Grim, then grabbed him in a hearty embrace.

While the men hugged, Billy stared at Uncle Grim's cloak. It was a wonder—when he reached out to touch it, his hand plunged through the black fabric into an elsewhere cold as a winter grave. The silver clasp was shaped like the skull-and-scales emblem of the Hall of Reception.

The emblem and cloak contained certain magics given only to higher officials. They improved Grim's ability to slip through the walls of this world, and the one between this world and the Afterlife. But Grim had also been entrusted with other powerful magics. He could stop time, a handy trick for anyone who needs to be in too many places at once. Grim also had the power to cut mortal threads.

He was a very busy skeleton. Grim was not only in charge of collecting all the expired human souls, his responsibilities included all nature's creatures, be it bug, boy or bear.

Grim Bones was in the fiftieth year of his three-hundred-year term as Head Field Agent for the Hall of Reception. Though he was relatively new to the job, he was already one of the most magical public servants in the Afterlife. He was surrounded by a blue glow.

'You two had better settle down before this closet gets turned upside down,' Mrs Bones's head shook between girlish amusement and motherly concern.

'Dear Decette, I see you have your hands full here.' Uncle Grim surveyed the jam-packed closet. 'Looks twice as full as the last time I saw it.'

'Yes, those Biglums are a dirty lot,' Mr Bones agreed as he untangled his watch chain.

Grim sighed heavily. 'Do you mind if Billy nips out for a visit with Fleggs? I think he's getting lonely.' The question was directed at Mr Bones, but Billy spun around to face his uncle. He had never been out of the closet before. Even one toe in the hall counted as a step closer to the outside world.

'Please!' squealed Billy. 'Oh can I?'

Mrs Bones pulled Billy close to her ridged chest. 'I'm not sure, Grim. Considering certain secrets . . .'

'Really, Decette.' Grim tried to hide a smile. 'No one will disturb Billy with Fleggs around, and he's much too smart to let the boy wander away.'

'I suppose you have a point.' She released Billy.

'That means I can go, right?' Billy skipped over to his father.

Mr Bones knelt down to look at him eye to eye. 'First you must promise me, Billy, that you'll be quieter than a whisper's whisper. There are people just beyond those walls. Do you understand?'

Had Billy's nod been any more enthusiastic, his head would have popped off his neck. 'Get on with you, then.' Mr Bones chuckled as Billy skipped into the dark passageway.

*   *   *

Grim Bones's square jaw and broad shoulder blades had always drawn more admiration than his brother's bookish looks. Grim approached life after death with a wide grin. This was the first time Mr Bones had ever seen concern pinch his brow bones.

Grim pulled the door almost shut, careful not to lock it. Secrets closets open only from the outside, making it even more difficult for skeletons to abandon their posts.

'Lars. Decette,' he whispered, 'I'm afraid we're in a pickle. There are rumours about matters here at the manor.'

'Of course, Grim. These Biglums are a scandal,' said Mr Bones.

'Yes, but the Righteousness Department wouldn't be disturbed by that sort of thing. They're used to all the typical human weaknesses. No, it's about your accepting an unacceptable shipment. Warehousing improper property.'

'Oh dear,' Mrs Bones gasped.

'Yes, quite. Oh dears all around.'

'But Grim, they're covered with official seals. Surely they can't blame us for accepting them?' Mr Bones gestured towards the trunks.

'High-ranking ghosts have been embarrassed,

you see, so I suspect they may try anything to pin the blame on someone else. Especially a lowly skeleton,' Grim said.

'We've had a request to keep these trunks secret.' Mr Bones glanced at his wife. She didn't look particularly happy with him at the moment.

'I trust you will keep that to yourselves. Right now, we must concern ourselves with the Investigative Branch's charges. They are pointing out that the trunks contain objects, not secrets. There's a big difference. If we start hiding *things* in closets instead of secrets, well, who knows what might show up! Murder weapons . . . bribes . . .'

Mr Bones crossed his arms with a *clack*. 'The Department of Fibs and Fabrications gives us some leeway in handling the unexpected. And these paintings certainly are!'

Grim slipped his arm around his brother's shoulders. 'Yes, most skeletons would agree with you. But the Afterlife is going through some unusual times—now that Pickerel and his Investigative Branch have become so powerful, and the Moral Authority approves everything he says.

'Somehow word has got out about your blunder, and Commissioner Pickerel is taking quite an interest. Have you two been talking to anyone?'

Mr Bones stepped away from Grim, eyes flashing. 'Blunder? We've accepted these trunks because there has been a request to keep them secret! And, *no,* we have *not* been talking to anyone. We wouldn't leave the closet!'

'I can't imagine old Mr Benders jumping up and down to turn himself in. Yet tongues are wagging, and if there's an investigation, it might lead to *our* little secret,' Grim fretted.

While the three of them talked, documents in a small brass box stirred and shuffled. The box was empty except for several documents relating to the secret in question, and all the emptier since a document had been removed years before. Grim strode over to the box, bent down, and picked it up. The secrets rattled inside, like a horde of bees banging on a window.

'There's enough in here to pack us all off to Nevermore,' continued Grim, 'even without the one I took for safe keeping.'

He placed the box back on the floor. Mr Bones frowned. Grim and Mr Bones had argued long and hard about removing that secret from the closet. Finally it was decided Grim could take the most incriminating secret, because it was the noisiest. The following years had been much quieter.

Grim Bones returned and placed a hand on his brother and sister-in-law's shoulders. 'With luck, things may quieten down. If not, I might have to do something about it.'

'What do you have in mind?' Mrs Bones murmured.

'I'd have to undo what I did long ago, Decette.'

'But we'd lose Billy!' she exclaimed.

Mr Bones clenched his jaw. 'We can't do that to the boy. Not after he's become so special to us, Grim.'

'Careful, brother.' Dark sparks cracked around Grim's glowing eyes. 'Let's hope for all our sakes the rumours fade away. Now I have to be off before the world population triples.' Grim swirled his cloak around his shoulders.

Fleggs pawed the floorboards outside the closet. Had he been other than a spirit horse the household would have thought itself under attack. As it was, his whinnies and stampings could barely be distinguished from the normal squeaks and bumps of an old mansion.

Billy had spent much of his visit patting Fleggs on the nose and whispering his secret wish to explore the seas. But, he confided, before setting sail, he'd be only too happy to gallop around the world on Fleggs's mighty back.

The secrets-closet door opened and Uncle Grim stepped out. He gave Billy a gentle pat on the head and swung into Fleggs's saddle.

'Are you coming back soon, Uncle Grim?' Billy asked.

'Hopefully not too soon, Billy. It's best if I don't.'

Billy was surprised at the abrupt end to his uncle's visit. He scrambled out of the way as Grim spun Fleggs around in the narrow passageway. Those in the Afterlife heard a deafening clatter of hooves, while those in life heard only a wind moaning towards some distant land.

Billy raised his hand to wave goodbye, but it was already too late. He lowered it slowly when he saw the anxious expression on his parents' faces.

CHAPTER 10

BIG, NASTY PLANS

'PRIMLY!' The shout erupted from the library and echoed through the manor, past indifferent statues and cringing maids, right into Miss Primly's ears. She stopped what she was doing (knocking two servants' heads together) and rushed to the library.

Before Sir Biglum's bellow died away, the sound of the housekeeper's heels tick-tacked into the library.

'Primly,' Sir Biglum fussed, 'I have a letter here for Messrs Hack, Whack and Plunder. Make SURE it gets into tomorrow's post!'

Sir Biglum rubbed his hands in greedy anticipation of a small fortune that would soon come his way. Supporting the gigantic manor required more money than the family's rapidly emptying vault had to offer. Especially with the bi-quadrennial Biglum ball coming up. Lord and

Lady Graspy of Fleeceham would be there, as would the Marquis Baguette of Bijou and the Grand Duke and Duchess of Ingot Hall. Even such notables as Waverly Cladbound, the shipping baron, and Florius Penwright, the author.

Surely this would be the year, at long last, that the cream of society would welcome the Biglums into their frothy upper circles. So what if his family had made its fortune through piracy? The Biglums had been outdoing themselves and everyone else for nearly a century, and Sir Biglum had sworn he'd carry on the family tradition of spending gold to buy respect. (It never occurred to him that the Biglums might have been accepted generations before, if they just hadn't been so disagreeably evil.)

Every two years, the ball put a fine cap on the social season. This year would be no exception. How embarrassing if it didn't outshine every other social gathering! For a moment, Sir Biglum wondered what new object he could showcase. Last time, his collection of jewel-encrusted Fabergé eggs had caused a sensation. He yearned for something truly special this year. He'd use it as bait. He had high hopes of marrying a rich young lady and her gold-spangled fortune.

But there was another reason he needed money. Sir Biglum had plans to build the world's largest factory.

A trickle of drool slicked Sir Biglum's lips as he thought of filling the factory with workers, plucked from cottages and farms around the manor and put to work day and night, grinding out a product sure to fly off store shelves.

And the source of this new fortune? The

fountainhead for all this untold wealth?

Tea cosies. Those padded cloth covers that keep teapots warm.

Made for pennies, sold for plump profits. He'd corner the market.

To make doubly sure that tea cosies would become all the rage, Sir Barkley Braggety Biglum VI had a devious plan. He was going to give away free samples of tea. And this tea would have some very interesting properties.

A nasty smile was followed by an even nastier chuckle as dark dreams washed over Sir Biglum. His team of scientists had perfected a substance called Begmoric Phosphate. Added to tea leaves, it blocked any tea drinker's ability to say, 'That's enough, thank you.' Instead, they would be on their knees pleading, 'More, more, more!'

He would call it Capital Tea. 'Today starts with Capital Tea!' People would drink it by the bucketful! And of course they'd want it hot, so he'd swoop in with his overpriced Capital Tea Brand Tea Cosies and gallon-sized teapots.

But there was one more piece to this plot, his absolute favourite: after everyone was hooked, he'd charge a small fortune for each tea bag!

A glowing green form spewed out of Sir Biglum's back and pounded him with congratulatory slaps. Greed was hooded and caped like most manifestations. But this one had been feeding on Sir Biglum's heart for so long, it was hard to tell where Sir Biglum started and the evil spectre left off. They shared a squat and malicious look.

Sir Biglum and Greed looked around the room. They had caught a faint whiff. 'Do you smell it?'

Sir Biglum asked his old companion. 'Smells like WEALTH. There's some kind of fortune connected to my niece. You know how well my nose appreciates the fine bouquet of MONEY . . . I've sensed it ever since she showed up.'

'Like a hog finding truffles,' Greed agreed. 'One of the many benefits of working with me.'

'It's hard to believe my pitiful brother-in-law could have owned anything of value. STILL . . . there's something. I've sent a note to my lawyers to investigate. And I'm having them look into another matter as well.'

CHAPTER 11

THE LESSON

For many hours Billy had been swinging from imaginary rigging and shouting pirate curses. Mr Bones had never seen him so filled with pirate fever. It had begun just after Scamp's visit, continued in earnest after Grim's departure, and lasted well into the night.

We really must have a bit more order in this closet, thought Mr Bones. *High time for lessons to begin.*

Mr Bones folded his paper, creasing it just so. 'Billy, my boy,' he declared, 'it's time we taught you something about secret keeping.' He knew he was taking a risk, secrets being such unpredictable things, especially in the hands of the unauthorized.

The words hit Billy like a cannonade salute. How long had he been waiting to hear that! His imaginary pirate ship slipped to the bottom of its imaginary sea.

'Flibbertigibbets!' Billy clapped his hands, and a

bright skeleton smile replaced his pirate scowl.

'Now, now, simmer down, my boy. You will have to pay close attention.' Mr Bones pulled up a spindly chair next to his own and motioned for Billy to sit down.

'Yes, *do* be careful, Billy,' Mrs Bones piped in. She turned to her husband. 'Are you really sure about this, Lars? We've had some nasty explosions in the past.'

'That was years ago, Decette. Besides, I'm just going over a few basics. Nothing too advanced.'

'Well, start with some small secrets, just in case,' she cautioned.

'Very sensible, my dear,' agreed Mr Bones. 'But before we dig into our secrets chests, let's set the stage . . .'

He rummaged around in his sleeping trunk and came up with a scuffed leather-bound book. It was titled: *The Secret Force Behind Secrets,* by Professor Drusus Deadbolt. Billy noticed someone had scrawled on the back in rounded script, filled with hearts and smiles: *You have the cutest grin.* It was signed: *Your lovey-dovey, Decette.*

Mr Bones slipped on his spectacles, then flipped the book over to see what Billy was staring at. 'Hrrrumph, yes well . . . quite . . . here we are: *The six theorems of secrets.* Now, my boy, these are the natural laws of secrets. Some of them you know and some of them will be new to you.'

Billy swallowed nervously and leaned forward. After years of waiting, the secrets of secret keeping were about to be his.

'*One,*' Mr Bones began. '*Secrets have a predisposition for revealing themselves. This has been proven many times over by using the formula*

70

$$\frac{S(MC^2)}{HT}$$

Or: Secrets times Mass, times Light Speed squared, divided by Hidden Truth.'

Mr Bones looked up and saw Billy's confused look. 'Hmm, perhaps we should forget the formulas and just concentrate on rules. This one's not particularly complicated: It's the basic nature of a secret to want to reveal itself.'

Billy nodded slowly, and Mr Bones continued. *'Two: It takes more energy to keep a secret than to share a secret.'* Mr Bones peered over the top of the book. 'I shouldn't think this would need much explanation. You've seen how much we fuss to keep them locked up and under control.'

Billy nodded with more assurance this time, and his dad read on. *'Three: The longer a secret remains a secret, the more energy it builds. This is called Retentive Energy.* Simple enough, eh? Now, Billy, these next three are a bit more complicated, so I'll explain them together. *Four: Dark secrets store and use more Retentive Energy than lighter secrets. Five: A secret will attempt to reveal itself whenever someone who is linked to the secret is nearby. Six: If a secret is exposed, it causes a terrible explosion, and can prompt other linked secrets to reveal themselves.'*

Mr Bones snapped the book closed, smiled, and slipped his arm around Billy's shoulders. 'Let's start with number four. Because secrets want to reveal themselves, they build up a kind of energy. That's not so hard to understand in plain English, eh?'

Billy smiled with relief. *This secrets business isn't so tough.* Mrs Bones smiled too. She was straightening the trunk blankets.

Mr Bones puffed up his ribcage with a fatherly pride at Billy's eagerness to learn. 'The next rule's not so difficult either. When a person who is linked to a secret is nearby, the secrets are attracted to him. Think of it as a kind of *magnetism*. And because secrets build on other secrets, they get linked together . . . and they get very powerful and difficult to handle.

'Now, this business about exposing secrets. A secrets keeper can reveal a secret by releasing it from his or her control, say, by opening a secrets trunk and letting it escape, or by reading the secret out loud.' He looked over his reading glasses with a tired smile. 'And we know all about that last one, now, don't we?'

Billy smiled weakly. 'Come on, Dad. I said I was sorry.'

'That you did . . . just trying to make a point. All this business about *secrets* . . . The same goes for *lies*.' Mr Bones tossed the book back in his sleeping trunk and brightened. 'Right. Now are you ready to double your knowledge?'

'Yes I *am*!' Billy nodded and leaned so far forward he nearly fell off his chair.

Mr Bones hopped up and clacked over to a stack of trunks. 'Then let's have a demonstration.' He examined the stack and opened the dustiest one. 'Here we are. It's a child's secret, so it shouldn't be too dangerous.' Mr Bones held up a light-coloured piece of parchment. The calfskin document was thick and mottled brown. It looked quite official to Billy. 'The first thing a secrets keeper needs to know is the class of document he's handling. That part is easy. See how light the parchment is? That tells you it's a rather ordinary secret. Had it been on dark parchment—'

'It would be a dark secret!' Billy broke in.

Mr Bones grinned at his wife. 'I think we've the makings of a top-level secrets keeper here, dear.' He tapped the document in the palm of his hand and continued the lesson. 'The grade of secret determines just how explosive it will be when the Oculus appears.'

'Is that the bright light that explodes the secrets?'

'Almost, my boy. That is the light of truth. The Oculus is a glowing hole between this world and the Afterlife that conducts the light.

'The next thing a secrets keeper needs to know is how to hold on to a secret.' Billy nodded, but as Mr Bones held up the document, it fluttered out of his hand and flew towards his son.

Before Billy had even touched the secret, the Oculus appeared and bathed him in light.

'BILLY!' both his parents shouted as he caught the document.

'Ooops!' Billy squeaked.

The document blasted apart, leaving all three skeletons coated in a fine ash. In the midst of the explosion, Billy saw a vision. It was through the eyes of a child, judging from the angle of the room and the pudgy hands and feet attached to the vision's point of view. He looked up to see another pudgy little boy hiding behind a doorway. This one was dressed identically, but smudged with a chocolate grin. There was something familiar about him.

Billy heard a woman's voice calling faintly, 'Where are you, dearest? Have you taken something you ought not to?'

'No, Mama.' The second boy giggled. He held a chocolate-coated finger to his lips and shushed the first boy to be quiet. Both voices were distorted, like they'd been trapped for years in a curtain of cobwebs.

The vision fell away.

'Criminy!' Billy cried and blew on his fingers. They tingled with hot sparks. Like any skeleton, Billy's sense of touch was as highly developed as his vision, so the explosion had been doubly painful.

'Fractured fibulae!' Mr Bones groaned. 'I'm forever mixing those two boys up!'

Mrs Bones glanced at her husband. 'Curious you picked that secret. You know it's linked to ours.'

Ours? Billy wondered.

Before the ash settled, a stack of trunks started to rumble and shake.

'Looks like the proper time has come, my dear.' Mrs Bones gestured towards the box. 'I don't think you'll find a better moment to tell him.'

Billy looked at his father, but Mr Bones seemed suddenly interested in examining his pipe. So Mrs Bones gave him a gentle nudge.

Mr Bones tapped his chin a few times with his ivory fingers. Billy stood up, his mouth open slightly, filled with unasked questions.

Mr Bones coughed a few times before finally starting. 'Billy, your mother and I have to talk to you about something important. Ahem. Urm. Well, you know we keep track of all these secrets; they come pouring in some days and other days they just come in dribs and drabs. You also know from personal experience how unpredictable they are. Yes, well . . .'

Mr Bones paused and examined his pipe once more. 'You may have assumed that secrets only belong to individuals who live outside this closet.' He looked at Mrs Bones, and she nodded back an encouraging smile. 'You see, Billy, not *all* of these secrets belong to outsiders. Some of them, just a few, mind you, belong to us.'

Billy blinked at his father and waited for him to continue.

The strongbox rattled again and glowed red. It lifted into the air and flopped into Mr Bones's lap. He grimaced and flipped open the lid. A dark document marked Top Secret skittered out of the box and floated in front of Mr Bones's face. The Oculus appeared again, flaring many times brighter than before and then—*BLAM!*—the secret exploded thunderously. Mr and Mrs Bones winced in pain. This time, Billy saw a long-ago vision through his father's eyes. His father was watching his mother and she looked like a protective angel as she hugged the same pudgy little boy.

Billy rubbed his eyes and looked again, but all that was left of the vision was smoke. The pain of the explosion had rattled Billy's teeth.

'Years ago, someone tossed you into this closet and locked the door,' Mr Bones said.

Mrs Bones added, 'We never saw who it was, sweetheart, but you were never going to get back out. The door only opens from the outside, and even Mr Benders wasn't about to come in, not with a human in here. You were surely going to—'

'We adopted you,' Mr Bones interrupted, then whispered to his wife, 'Let's avoid the gruesome details for now. It looks like he's not taking this

75

too well.'

Two more Top Secret documents sprang in the air. *BLAM BLAM! Ouch ouch!* Again, Billy saw a brief vision, this time through the eyes of Mrs Bones. He watched as his father sang gently to a young skeleton and cradled him in his arms. He recognized himself, but wondered what had become of the live boy.

He had no memory of any of this. As far as he knew, he had always lived in this closet with them. His world was looking very wobbly as his eyes filled with foggy tears.

'Come here, my Billy.' Mr Bones pulled Billy on to his lap, wrapping him in a bony hug and rocking him gently. 'Billy, I know we never really talk about this sort of thing. It's a hard old habit from keeping secrets day in and day out. But you need to know that we've always loved you as our own son. I hope you've felt that.'

Mr Bones tightened his hug. Billy nodded sadly. Now that the basic secrets were exposed, Mr and Mrs Bones could fill in the details without additional explosions.

Mrs Bones stroked the top of Billy's smooth head. 'I know this a bit of a shock, Billy. Would you like to talk about this later?'

Billy pulled his knees up to his chest and allowed himself to be rocked. It was an eloquent answer to Mr and Mrs Bones.

'We'll talk when you're ready. No rush. We have all the time in the world, and then some. Just relax.'

She lifted Billy up and brought him over to his sea chest. She wiped his face clean with a dust rag, patted him with a towel, and helped him slip on his old nightshirt. 'All right, Billy-pumpkin, get some sleep now.'

Billy pulled his horse blanket up and snuggled deeper into his sea chest. Mr and Mrs Bones each gave him a kiss and hovered over the bed until he drifted off. They tiptoed away, hoping he would find some peace in a night's rest.

It wasn't going to be as much rest as they had hoped, because just as they settled into their own trunk, there was a murmur outside, and then a scraping at the keyhole. The lock turned with a timid squeak and the door creaked open.

CHAPTER 12

DIRTY DISHES DOWNSTAIRS

Every clock in the manor struck the quarter hour. It sounded like there were hundreds. Millicent heard the clanging chorus announce a quarter to ten. She tucked Helen into bed, lit her beeswax candle, and slipped the matchbox into her sleeve. The candle flickered nervously as she thumped heavily down the dark servant stairwell. This was the first night of her two-night sentence in the scullery. The damp basement washroom was the most horrid room in the house.

The happiness she'd felt from meeting her grandmother melted away when she entered the kitchen. As grand as High Manners Manor was from the front, the kitchen was remarkably small and decrepit. No expense was spared where it could impress important people, but Biglum pinched pennies until they screamed everywhere else in the house.

In the service rooms, the knotty pine cabinets were warped and wobbly. The unpainted plaster walls were covered in soot. And, especially in the summer, the heat was enough to cook food before it hit the stove. Millicent's curls withered like lettuce leaves as soon as she stepped into the room.

Cook sat at the centre table grunting orders to her two assistants. She reminded Millicent of a pig. Her mean little grey eyes spied Millicent entering the room.

While Cook's attention was turned, her two assistants dropped a heavy pot.

'Oooooooh, you brainless nincompoops!' she squealed. 'How'd you manage that? That's the second pot you two overturned today. Get the mops out and clean it up! You too, you little attic rat!'

Millicent knew to jump in and help, or she wouldn't get a scrap of food. The three scrubbed up as much kidney stew as they could, and eventually the floor looked presentable again.

Millicent rinsed out the mops in the back hall work sink and put them away in a tumbledown cupboard. When she returned, she heard one of the assistant cooks complaining. 'It's her, I tell you. She gave us a shock when she poked her head into the kitchen.'

The first assistant jerked her head at Millicent and then the second one lit in. 'Things haven't been the same since she moved to the manor. Used to be settled and peaceful . . . almost boring. The place is pandemonium now.'

Millicent had heard it before. It had become a game with the nastier members of the staff: 'Pin

79

the Blame on Millicent.'

Cook whacked a wooden spoon on the edge of a pot. 'Right then, Miss Attic Rat, you'd better get cracking with those dishes.'

The assistants were careful to hide their smirks as they removed their slop-soaked aprons and fled. Millicent sighed. Every available spot in the kitchen was stacked with dirty pots, cutlery and plates from Sir Biglum's evening feast and the large staff's modest dinner. There was also a surprisingly high stack of teacups and a huge teapot.

Cook sat on her well-worn stool, impatiently tapping her spoon. 'Get the dishes all downstairs in the dumb waiter, then you can wash them up in the scullery. Now! Break anything and I won't be gentle with the rolling pin, I promise you.'

Millicent lifted a heavy stack of filthy tableware into the cabinet-size lift and lowered it to the washing room in the basement. Then she trotted down the stairs, unloaded, ran back up and repeated the whole dumb-waiter operation again.

Millicent was tired to the bone before she had scrubbed one dish. Cook, meanwhile, was dead to the world. She lay in a toppled heap on the centre table, four empty bottles of cooking sherry beside her, snoring loudly.

Downstairs, the scullery was dimly lit by a small gas flame over the large porcelain work sink. The rest of the room was plain as plaster with exposed copper pipes and a sturdy table to hold the mountain of dishes.

There was plenty of hot water. The manor's water was always steaming hot, and even the cold water was warm. Miss Primly's crew slaved around the clock, firing the boilers to supply the manor with heat and hot water. Millicent could hear them several dingy hallways away as they struggled to shovel coal into the belching flames.

As Millicent ran hot water into the deep sink, she heard a loud *BOOM!* It was not far from where she stood. The storage closet under the scullery stairs blew open.

The closet was empty aside from cobwebs and dust. On the back wall, tucked under the empty shelves, a thin rectangular wall panel had blown open as well. Without hesitation, Millicent grabbed her candle and squeezed through the panel opening. She found herself in a narrow passage layered with dust and grit.

She crawled along on her hands and knees. Dust tickled her nose. The cramped tunnel ended abruptly at another hinged panel. She inched through and found that she could stand up. Millicent was in a very narrow and completely dark passageway. From what she could see, the hallway was constructed from rough wood. She held the candle in front of her, illuminating a staircase. She followed it up.

Something wisped across her cheek. A cold shiver ran from her heels right up her neck. Her hands trembled as she clawed at her face. Cobwebs drifted down from the wall over her head and shoulders. She pulled frantically, banging an elbow into a beam.

Millicent winced and cradled her arm. When she looked up again, she noticed paired holes poking dim light through the wall above and a series of wooden crossbars extending down. She rubbed away the last of the tingles, then hitched up her skirt in an unladylike manner and pulled herself up the crude ladder. Hooking her arm around the top bar, Millicent looked through the holes, and discovered a view of the dining room.

A long mahogany table paraded down the centre of the wood-panelled dining room. Three ornate chandeliers floated above. They dripped with darkened crystal like the Queen of Ice hung by her heels.

A lone place setting at the end of the table waited patiently for tomorrow's breakfast.

Millicent carefully climbed back down. A door disguised as a sideboard was set into the wall, next to the ladder.

To Millicent Hues, expert explorer and curiosity seeker, this explore had been better by half than anything she could have dreamt of. After all the time stuck twiddling her thumbs in the attic, she was thrilled to be on the trail of a mystery. Who had built these dark passages and what was their secret use? She entered the dining room, closing the sideboard-door behind her. She counted fifty chairs on each side of the table. The gold-leafed chair at the end was like a throne, at least two heads taller than the others, with an ivy design twisting up its back. Millicent *had* to try it out. She scrambled under the table and up into the seat. Imagining herself the Grand Duchess of Houndstooth-on-Codswattle, she picked up a silver spoon and held it up to her eye, pretending it was an opera glass.

'How do you do m' Lord?' she said to herself as she bowed to one side. 'How are you this evening, my dear Countess?' She bowed to the other side. 'Blinking bogies!'

Millicent slipped the spoon back and scooted under the table. The room's double doors opened with twin *kabooms*. Millicent nervously pinched her candle out and waited.

A pair of stubby legs, clothed in dark blue pinstriped trousers and patent leather shoes, entered the room and marched up the length of the table. The legs stopped. One shiny shoe tapped impatiently, and Millicent heard an equally impatient sniff. The legs were about to leave the room when they slowed and then paused by the sideboard.

With a small grunt, the leg's owner opened the sideboard door. Millicent closed her eyes and held still until the legs departed through the double doors.

A few minutes later, Millicent crept from under the table and back into the passageway.

Millicent rolled the door shut, and pressed her back to the wall to recover. She listened to make sure all was quiet, then relit her candle and continued into the darkness. The passageway widened. Millicent crept forward. After only a few paces, her candlelight caught the edges of a door.

Carved into the thick stonework trim were intertwined scrolls, skulls and balancing scales. In the centre of the arch, a large skull looked down expectantly. A gold doorknob winked at Millicent in the candlelight. She gave it a tentative twist, but the door was locked.

Next to the huge door, a skeleton key hung from a sign. It read: 'Tell a truth.'

Millicent tried to remove the key, but it too wouldn't budge. She backed up to look at the door again. Worked into the sandstone trim around the top of the door were more words. 'The truth will set us free.'

Millicent thought for a moment and spoke the first truth that popped into her mind. 'Miss Primly is a horrid old crow.' The key shimmered with a purple glow, wriggled off the sign, and leaped into the keyhole. Millicent carefully turned the key. The door creaked open.

Millicent stepped into the room, holding her candle high. The first sound to greet her was a loud gasp. She saw two skeletons sitting up in a large wooden trunk. The one with the frilly nightcap jerked the bedclothes up and uncorked a bone-chilling scream.

Millicent fainted with a *thump*.

13

INTRODUCTIONS

Mrs Bones was the first to recover. She hopped out of the trunk and clacked over to Millicent.

'Oh dear, I'm so sorry!' Mrs Bones apologized. 'I'm always startled by the living. Can you forgive me?' She caressed Millicent with a motherly hand.

Millicent jammed her eyes shut (intending never to open them again), but Mrs Bones's flute-like voice finally brought her around. She peeped one brown eye open, then the other.

Millicent was topping records for seeing what ought not to be there. But, on a second look, these skeletons weren't so scary. They had the loveliest eyes, like blue moon glow. And their toothy smiles were rather sweet.

'That's it, my dear,' Mrs Bones whispered.

Billy was as startled as Millicent by the scream. He popped out of his trunk and hugged the back of Mr Bones's legs while the older skeleton placed the key back on its hook.

Mr Bones bowed and offered Millicent his bony hand. 'I guess you're young Millicent Hues. Have I the pleasure?'

Millicent was baffled they knew her, then thought, *I really shouldn't be surprised by anything in this odd house.*

'Welcome to our humble home,' continued Mr Bones. 'You'll have to be careful in here, it's close quarters, I'm afraid. My name is Mr Bones and this is Mrs Bones. And this,' he looked over his shoulder, 'is Billy.'

Millicent and Billy both leaned curiously around Mr Bones's nightshirt and met each other's glances.

'Come on lad, don't be afraid.' Mr Bones scooted Billy forward. 'She's only a girl. The world out there is full of them. Maybe someday you'll see for yourself.'

Mrs Bones smiled at seeing the two children together. They were cute as two kittens in cream. But then her eye landed on the tumble of trunks from the night's explosions.

'Oh!' she gasped. 'Look at the mess!' Mrs Bones's fingers clattered on her cheeks. 'How embarrassing! Why don't you help me straighten up a bit while the children get to know one another,' she said to her husband.

They withdrew to the trunks on the other side of the closet, leaving the two children to eye each other. Millicent's were wide with worry, and Billy's glowed with wonderment. He was the first to let curiosity prod him forward. 'What's it like . . . the world out there?'

'I'm not sure,' Millicent said. 'I've never seen

86

the whole world—just little bits of it. Mostly in the city where I used to live with my mother and father.'

The young skeleton in the oversized nightshirt smiled brightly.

This was a sight beyond anything Millicent had imagined she'd come across in any explore. But she had to admit, despite his clattering bones, he seemed a lot like a porcelain doll. His face was so smooth and his expression so sweet. 'Haven't you ever been outside this closet?' she asked.

'Nah. Except for the hallway, but that doesn't count for much,' Billy said casually. Stepping into the hallway the night before had been a thrill, but this girl with the runaway hair and candlelit eyes had been to so many more places. 'Been here forever, I think. My parents have been assigned here a very long time.' And for a few moments, Billy wondered how long, and how many secrets they knew, especially about him. 'We're a pretty nice family, I think, once you get to know us. Want to meet Scamp?'

Billy clattered back to his sea chest and produced the shiny black beetle. Scamp bowed with a flourish. Millicent was immediately taken with the beetle's chivalry and eager to have him run around on her palm.

Scamp chittered something unintelligible to Millicent. She looked at Billy in confusion.

'Oh.' Billy grinned. 'He says he thinks you're much nicer than the other humans outside. *They're* always rushing around trying to squash him.'

'I know how he feels.' Millicent curtsied to the little bug and then handed him back. This was a curious place, indeed, but the kindness she felt in

87

this snug closet warmed her like a goose-down blanket.

Scamp scuttled up Billy's arm and rested on his shoulder. It was the bug's favourite seat. Millicent looked around at the stacked trunks and the others that Mr and Mrs Bones were rearranging. 'What are all these for?'

'Mostly lies, but lots of secrets too.'

'Really? Whose lies? And look how many!'

Billy chuckled. 'It's not nearly half of them. The worst of the worst are pressed tight in the strong boxes, over there. My parents are always going on about these horrible Biglums.'

'But why are they here?'

Billy told her a few basics about secrets closets and skeletons. Afterwards, the children fell into an awkward silence as Millicent struggled to take all of these oddities in. Scamp shifted on Billy's shoulder, prompting the skeleton's next thought. 'Scamp tells me the rest of this house is very large and fancy. What kind of room are you staying in? Is it like a palace?'

'A palace!' Millicent giggled, thinking of her bleak bedroom. 'More like a shack.'

'It can't be all that bad. Anything's got to be better than this stuffy old closet. I'd give anything to see it.'

'It's not very impressive, I promise you.'

'There's got to be something good about it,' Billy insisted.

Millicent had to think for a moment, then remembered. 'It has quite a nice view.'

She went on to describe it at length, but no detail was too small for Billy.

When she mentioned the rolling green fields, he

demanded to know more. 'What about the grass? Is each blade the same colour? What happens when you walk on it? Does it feel pain, make sounds, or talk like people?'

Millicent struggled to hide a smile. *He has the oddest questions.* She patiently explained as much as she knew on the subject of grass. When she finished, she had a few questions of her own. 'Seeing how you're dead and all, you must know loads about the Afterlife.'

Billy bit where his bottom lip should have been. 'Wish I did. I do know a *few* things.'

Millicent closed her eyes wistfully. 'When I think about dead people, I imagine them sitting up there on clouds, with white-feathered wings and harps.'

This time it was Billy's turn to cover his smile. 'Well . . . they could do those sorts of things if they really wanted to . . . but there are much more interesting ways to spend your time. Like living in a house made of moonbeams, or summoning up a bagpipe band instead of plunking on a silly old harp. And I'm afraid feathery wings are reserved for pretty high-ranking officials. The ones in the Realms Above.'

Scamp nodded wisely, as if to say he'd heard as much from Mr Benders.

'Not many wear them these days. Feathers have gone out of style.' Billy smiled.

'I was only wondering, because my parents are dead,' Millicent said sadly.

Billy gently touched her shoulder and whispered, 'Well, as you can see, so are mine.'

Millicent smiled, despite herself. Maybe she and this new young friend had a lot in common, apart from the humdrum differences like his being dead and her being alive. It was awfully nice to talk to someone her own age.

She was still curious about skeletons and took the chance to ask more questions. She learned: 'Official Secret Keeper Skeletons never get out of the closet while they're stationed on Earth . . . unless their assigned family moves to a new house. Of course, I'd be free to wander the world, if I could ever get out of here, because my parents are official keepers, not me.' Billy also told her: 'We love hot cocoa, but we don't need to eat.' And it took very little conversation to find out that Billy dreamed most of all to explore the world as a fearless pirate.

Billy found out that Millicent's favourite food was goose and gravy and she adored big breakfasts in bed, her favourite music was opera (she and her father used to walk at night and listen from behind the great hall as the soprano's voice sailed to the heavens or plunged into mournful sobs), and her favourite colour was definitely not black. Millicent could hardly wait for her mourning period to be over, so she could slip on a bold red corduroy dress. Billy also learned what Millicent loved most: explores and solving mysteries.

Which greatly interested Billy, because of the healthy sized mystery that had recently landed in his lap.

They talked for hours and would have talked for days if they could have.

Their conversation finally slowed down when Millicent yawned and looked at the door. But before she could begin her goodbyes, one more question tumbled out of Billy's mouth. 'Do you think I could come with you?'

At first, Millicent didn't know what to say. But the more she thought about it, the more she liked the idea.

Billy fidgeted while he waited for her reply. What if his best chance to see the world got up and walked out of the door!

'I won't take up much room,' he pleaded.

Finally, Millicent smiled. 'Of course you can come. I only have my doll Helen up there . . . she won't mind the extra company.'

So it was settled between the two new friends. Billy nearly danced with excitement (a sight that could have given any normal person the shivering shimmies, but not Millicent).

In only a few hours, their friendship had grown thick as Cook's plum pudding. Millicent hadn't been this happy since she'd first met Vanessa. Billy had never been this happy. *Skiffs and skittles! A friend my own age. And I don't even have to speak to her in Bug!*

Excitement was a rare commodity for Billy, but one he had recently developed a taste for—first with the appearance of the trunks, then with surprise visits of Uncle Grim and Fleggs, and now this new friend. Billy remembered, with more excitement, the paintings and the letter. He clomped over to the three trunks and busied himself with the latches.

He flipped up the first lid. Millicent's eyes opened wider than the trunk. 'Those are my father's paintings!'

'They are indeed,' said Mr Bones, returning from the opposite side of the closet. 'That reminds me . . .' He retrieved the claims form from the walnut filing cabinet and handed it to Millicent. 'You'll need this if you ever want to remove the paintings.'

Millicent carefully tucked the document in her sleeve and asked, 'How'd they get in here?'

'Mr Benders delivered them on his last run from the Afterlife,' Billy explained. He looked at his father. 'Can Millicent read the letter?'

Mr Bones nodded slowly. 'It's irregular, but I don't see any harm. It's not an official DFF document.'

He leafed through one of the trunks and pulled out the letter, which he handed to Millicent. She read it in silence and could almost hear her father's pen scratching the paper. The letter shook softly in her hands, and her eyes glistened. She folded it back up and looked at Mr Bones. 'Can I keep it? It's my father's handwriting.'

Mr Bones gently retrieved the letter. 'That, I think, would be going too far. I'll tuck it back into the trunk until you can safely remove the paintings.'

Millicent stared down at the rows of rough planks lined up along the floor. The Boneses waited patiently while she collected herself.

Billy broke the silence. 'I want to go with her. I want to see the outside world!'

Mr and Mrs Bones's heads snapped up. Worry filled their luminous eyes. Then Millicent shyly spoke. 'I could use a hand. If I don't get the dishes done, Cook's going to starve me to death for sure. There's a mountain of them back there.'

Billy's parents paled to a brighter white, not sure if she was exaggerating.

Mrs Bones glanced at her husband. 'It's his

chance to get out, dear. It might be a long time before he gets another.'

Mr Bones popped his pipe from his mouth. 'I'll tell you what, you two. Let's try it for a day and see what happens. But you need to check in with us tomorrow night. We'll take this a little at a time.'

'You must stay out of the way of the living, dear. Promise me?' Mrs Bones's motherly concern filled her words.

Billy agreed, and probably would have promised to hop on one leg for the whole time, if it meant getting to the outside world. Millicent, on the other hand, felt she was going to miss this odd place.

Billy's parents delivered bone-smushing hugs to each child, then Billy and Millicent were off to the scullery. While Scamp rode on the skeleton like a tiny parrot on a pirate's shoulder, Billy swivelled his head this way and that, even in a full circle, as only skeletons can.

Many people would find the scullery an awful place to work, what with its damp, mould and endless stacks of dishes, but Billy was fascinated. The wet ash smell of lye and laundry drying on suspended racks; the peeling whitewashed walls puckered from years of steamy air. Billy was particularly taken with the long-handled scrubbing brush and differing shades of green on the copper pipes and taps. When he saw Sir Biglum's mountain of cups and saucers, he was convinced the living must like their tea as much as they liked breathing.

Once Billy focused on the dishes, he was a great help. He worked tirelessly, an advantage of not having any muscles. Millicent had to nudge him a few times as he stared into the rainbow on a soap bubble. They stopped for a water fight just once—and the job mostly went quick as bug blinks.

Just as they were finishing up, Millicent asked Billy the question that had been eating away at her ever since she had first come down to the scullery. 'What were those explosions, Billy?'

Billy wasn't eager to talk about it—the pain of finding out he was adopted was too fresh. But Millicent insisted, and he finally gave in. 'It was the light of truth exploding some secrets.'

Exploding secrets! One more wonder stacked on to all these others. She dried a blue china teacup and placed it on top of the rest. 'They must have been pretty big secrets. I heard the blasts all the way from here.'

'Come to think of it, the documents were pretty dark.' Billy nodded thoughtfully. 'That's unusual . . . being my parents' secrets and all.'

'Ooh, your parents have secrets! What were they, Billy?'

He didn't want to talk about it, but he was so horrid at keeping anything hidden, he launched into an explanation of the explosions and visions.

'Oh, Billy, this sounds like a real mystery! I'm glad you told me. We'll have to get to the bottom of it right away.'

Billy felt cut straight down the middle. One side was reeling from not knowing who he really was. The other side wanted very much to know who had tossed him in the closet to die.

It was a wonderful thing that Millicent had arrived to help straighten things out. Especially now that he was out of his closet, and in the real world! If he had any skin he would have pinched it

94

to make sure he wasn't dreaming. He gave Millicent a crescent-moon grin.

Millicent tried to stifle a tremendous yawn, unsuccessfully. 'Maybe we should start on this mystery tomorrow.' She dried and stacked the last gold-trimmed plate.

Now there was only the matter of getting back up to the attic. Millicent wasn't worried about the servants: they'd be long in bed by now. But she wasn't so sure about Cook. The kitchen table wasn't the best place for a good night's rest, so the old sot might be stirring.

Billy skipped to the stairs and clattered up a few steps.

'Hang on, Billy,' Millicent warned. 'Last time I saw Cook, she was snoring like two handsaws, but that kind of racket will wake her.'

Billy froze. *Squids and squalls! Out in the world for such a short time, and already making bone-headed mistakes!* He promised himself to do better. He grabbed the thin banister and practised creeping around. From his perch on the skeleton's shoulder, Scamp squeaked out a few tips. But they mostly involved scuttling under floorboards and behind walls, so they weren't entirely helpful.

Billy sighed. 'Even if she sees us, maybe she'll forget by morning.'

'Or, maybe—' a sly smile circled Millicent's mouth—'I can pretend you're not there. She won't know if you're real or part of her imagination.'

'I'll pretend I'm a white elephant,' Billy laughed, waving one arm in front of his face like a trunk.

'Even better! Then I'll say, "What's the matter? It's just me and my elephant friend." And we'll walk out of the kitchen, like nothing could be more normal.'

They had to wait out a fit of giggles before getting under way. Minutes later, they slipped past Cook, still snoring. They were quiet as mice in silk slippers.

Afterwards, Billy was a little disappointed they hadn't needed to pull off the plan, but he knew it was just as well, and his parents would have agreed.

Once upstairs, he settled into Millicent's empty trunk, but couldn't close his eyes. It took a long time before he surrendered this dream-come-true for an actual dream.

CHAPTER 14

A NEW FRIEND AND AN OLD LOSS

'More kippers, dear?' Dame Biglum asked Millicent. They were seated together in her cheery bedroom. Martha had brought up a marvellous breakfast of boiled eggs, herring, lashings of toast and tart orange marmalade. Millicent had barely said a word all morning. Her mouth had been too full. But she knew there was plenty to say about her new friend.

She thought she should approach the subject cautiously, so as not to scare her grandmother. She had asked Billy to hide in one of the attic storage rooms filled with mothballed clothes, hatboxes and old furniture. It was just down the dark hallway from her grandmother's room. Millicent hoped he wasn't getting too restless while she was devouring toast and eggs.

*   *   *

Billy *was* getting restless—twitchy as a whip flick, really. He sent Scamp to look out. When the bug reported the coast was clear, Billy scooped him up and wandered out into the hall.

He was about halfway to the playroom when he heard a woman humming. He nipped back into the storage room just as Martha clattered into the hallway with the dirty breakfast dishes. She passed Billy and headed down the stairs. A moment later Billy entered the playroom.

He was immediately drawn to the wondrous old toys. The chestnut brown rocking horse was particularly alluring (not as impressive as Fleggs, but still a proud steed). Billy pulled the horse's wooden head towards him. It bowed a royal greeting, then reared up into a warhorse's stance. It was too much to resist. He was up and rocking at once. A small thread of a memory unspooled in his mind.

Billy rocked wildly, shouting, 'The King's men will show you no mercy!'

'BILLY! Be quiet! You'll scare the dickens out of Grandmother! I haven't told her about you yet!'

As Billy turned to look over his shoulder, the great horse pitched him forward. He flew off, bumped his head on the wall, then clattered to the floor. Pieces of Billy scattered across the room.

He blinked, then tumbled his head upright. His hands skittered across the floor on fingertips and reattached to his arms. He rebuilt his body a piece at a time, finally crawling over on bony hands and knees to fetch his head. (Young skeletons are trained almost as soon as they can walk for such a situation. They spend hours disassembling and reassembling themselves, blindfolded. And because there aren't many distractions in a secrets closet, they often use body parts the way living children build with blocks.)

Millicent nearly dropped her own jaw and forgot to warn her grandmother. Dame Biglum entered the playroom just as Billy stood up and rolled his head around, making sure it was firmly attached. Her cane clattered to the floor. She grabbed Millicent's shoulder and wheezed in a sharp breath.

But instead of falling over in a dead faint, she thrust out her chin bravely and said, 'I see you've finally come for me. I *do* thank you for not coming a few days before, or I wouldn't have had the chance to meet this wonderful young person.'

Tears shone on the old woman's cheeks as she patted Millicent's shoulder. 'Take me to the Afterlife. I'm ready.' She stepped forward, arms outstretched.

Billy and Millicent looked at her like she was loony.

'Grandmother?' Millicent spoke up timidly, 'This is Billy. He's my new friend. He lives downstairs with his parents in the secrets closet.' Millicent retrieved her grandmother's silver-capped cane and handed it back to her.

'Billy? Secrets closet? Eh? Oh, I'll be a pickle, dilled and dotty. Thought I had a one-way ticket to the other side.' She motioned to Billy. 'I'm dizzy. Do you mind if we sit down in my room?'

*   *   *

Soon Billy and Millicent were sitting on the sofa

99

opposite Dame Biglum. Her heart had finally slowed from a *thumpity tump* to a more regular *lump dump*. 'I'm sorry, m'dears, I was sure you were the Grim Reaper.' She tipped her cane handle towards Billy.

'Oh, you thought I was Uncle Grim. No, he's much taller than I am. And, I think, more handsome.'

Millicent burst in, 'Go on! You know the Grim Reaper?' She bounced so hard on the couch it coughed crankily.

'Well, I think I should,' Billy said proudly. 'He *is* my uncle. He visits my family's closet a few times a year, mostly around the holidays. He says he doesn't get as much business when families celebrate together. And he's got the most wonderful horse.' Billy paused for a moment. 'But Uncle Grim and Fleggs never stay long. They're very busy.'

'Yes, I expect they are,' returned Dame Biglum. She sensed something oddly familiar about the little skeleton, especially his soft blue eyes and the way he leaned in his chair with no sense of proper posture. There was also the way he swung his feet when he talked.

While Dame Biglum studied Billy, Millicent was up and out of her seat, poking around the room. She stopped at her grandmother's chest of drawers. Plopping her elbows down, she examined the pictures displayed there. 'Who are these twin boys? And this looks like my mum.'

Dame Biglum snapped her fan shut and sighed. 'Those are pictures of my children. The girl is your mother . . . my youngest. The boys . . . well, that's a longer tale. They were born in the identical hour,

100

on the identical day and year. There were never two more identical twins. I'm embarrassed to say that even I couldn't tell them apart.

'All three children were a perfect delight, rather surprising when you consider the shivery nature of this house and their dreadful father Sir Biglum the Fifth. But, about the age of ten, one of my sons began to turn bad. It started with little things like sneaking chocolate and hoarding crumb cakes, but steadily grew to snatching silverware and antique china. There were even complaints from the staff that someone was pinching jewellery.

'About that time, one boy disappeared. We searched endlessly but never saw a sign of him again.' Billy examined Dame Biglum's face. She closed her eyes briefly and took a deep breath. 'His name was Goodwin. Goodwin William Biglum . . . the poor lost soul. Barkley, the firstborn and heir, survived. And he soured into the sorry man you see today. Believe me, it's embarrassing to have failed so completely as a parent. Lost one child then watched the other ruined by this dreadful house . . . Just as every Sir Biglum has been, one through six.

'Millicent, it's no wonder your mother wanted to flee. I only wish I had her strength, so I could have joined her.' Dame Biglum banged her cane on the floor. 'I often curse the day I married into *this* family. It has surely been a curse on me.'

The memories had clearly taken a toll on the old woman. When she had finished, she sat silently. Her eyes were cloudy again, and she seemed to shrink as she settled back into her chair.

Billy felt sorry for her. He understood only too well what it was like to be locked up, and the old woman looked trapped inside herself.

It was lucky that the conversation lulled, because Martha came down the hallway just then. Billy scarcely had time to scoot into Dame Biglum's wardrobe.

When Martha gathered herself and knocked on Dame Biglum's door, her words were mixed with panting breaths. 'Excuse me, Madam . . . but . . . Miss Pri . . . the housekeeper wanted me to take Miss Millicent downstairs. She's got . . . a new chore . . . for her.'

Dame Biglum bowed her head.

'She wants Millicent working at sewing cloth tea bags . . . Has a stack that needs stitching, she said.'

Millicent sighed. She wasn't worried about getting the job done in time: she was handy with needle and thread. But she was worried about her grandmother.

'I'll be back in no time, Grandma Maddy. Don't worry.' Millicent used as reassuring a tone as she could muster. She squeezed the old woman's careworn hand.

Dame Biglum frowned and her soft blue eyes flashed. 'That woman will be the end of me, for sure.' After a moment, she returned Millicent's squeeze and added, 'I'm so sorry, my dear. Get that tiresome job done as quickly as possible. I want you back here for my own greedy reasons.'

Millicent hugged the old woman. As she waved goodbye to her grandmother, she shot another glance at the wardrobe.

CHAPTER 15

THE SEA CHEST

Inside the wardrobe, Billy pressed into the arms of several fur coats, puffy-sleeved dresses and lacy shawls. He could barely hear the muffled conversation outside; it reminded him of secrets stirring inside a trunk. While he waited, he mulled over the tale of the lost twin. He was starting to wonder if he had more than a little to do with the mystery.

Dame Biglum spotted Billy peeking out of the wardrobe. 'Billy, it's well past time you should be out of that nightshirt. Why don't we find some daywear, eh?'

The old woman lit an oil lamp and led Billy to a storage room. 'These were the twins' clothes from the time of Goodwin's disappearance.' She rooted around in a trunk and pulled out an old velvet and lace sailor suit. 'This should do nicely.' She held the suit up to check the size.

Billy stepped out of his nightshirt and pulled on the sailor suit, along with some dusty boots. He thought that he looked rather dashing.

'Is this what pirates used to wear?' he asked Dame Biglum. 'Someday I want to sail the seven seas and be a buccaneer!' He raised an imaginary sword to the sky. His stockings flopped down on his buttoned-up boots.

Dame Biglum examined him closely. 'That's an unusual calling to have,' she commented, 'but not for this family. What on Earth made you say it?'

Billy explained that the trunk he had slept in for years still contained remnants of old sea stories.

'Remarkable.' Dame Biglum's eyes shrouded in mist.

Billy wandered over to a crude cabinet holding a large clockwork train. It was as big as a bulldog, had a tall smokestack mounted on a tubby green cylinder, and six cogged wheels. When he looked at it longingly, Dame Biglum chuckled and told him to have a go. Billy clomped down on his knees and wound it up. After all the years, it was still in good repair. The train chugged across the floor and Billy scrambled after it. Dame Biglum excused herself for a small nap.

On the hundredth time the train trundled away, Billy was finally losing interest. But on its last run, the train bumped into a cabinet at the far end of the room. The crash was followed by a clicking sound. A narrow crack opened between the cabinet and the wall.

Adventure beckoned Billy, like a distant pirate's song. He pulled at the edge with the thin tips of his finger bones. A door creaked open. Scamp, who had been hitching a ride on Billy's shoulder, squeaked in surprise. 'Looks like a secret staircase,' Billy told his insect friend. 'Let's have a look.'

He ducked in, closing the door behind them. The inside of a coal sack wouldn't have been blacker, but the two of them had eyes equipped for the dark. The bony and buggy explorers made their way carefully down the steep stairwell.

Deep below, a maze of interconnecting passageways led to a winding cave. Scamp squeaked that it looked familiar from his gravy misadventure. Billy tingled with a mix of nerves and excitement. The beetle called out directions and soon they found the cell-like room that housed the chest.

Billy looked it over and agreed with Scamp that it looked like a match for Billy's bed. He put his earhole up to one side of the chest. A voice murmured inside.

Billy found the trunk's clasps. As he tried to prise them open, he accidentally tipped the trunk. Something clattered inside.

As Billy bent forward for a better grip, the room lit up with a ghostly blue glow. 'I'd lay a bet them clasps will be rusted tight by now,' said a sea-salted voice. A parrot squawked, Billy bolted upright, and Scamp flipped in fright.

Billy recognized the voice straight away. It was the same one he'd heard mixed up in the memories of his own sea chest. Excitement danced in his bones.

The old pirate stood with his legs embedded in the trunk. He was dressed in an outfit of translucent blue, a long coat with lacy cuffs, and pantaloons clasped just below his knees. A thick belt held a vicious sword and scabbard. One eye had a shrewd twinkle. The other was made of glass. The ghost parrot on his shoulder fluffed and preened.

Billy was fascinated. Standing next to a real pirate, long dead or not—well, it was like looking for a penny in your pocket and finding a gold doubloon!

'Yer a fine lad for freeing me.' The ghost tried to straighten up. 'Fishtails and narwhals! Feels like a four-pound ball's been fired into me backside. Give me a hand, boy, so I can raise sail.'

Billy offered his hand, and the ghost grabbed at it. His hand passed through Billy's a few times before it solidified. The little skeleton pulled the ghost upright.

'There's a lad.' The ghost nodded and touched his hat. Its wide brim was bent up in front and topped with a long soft feather. 'Name's Glass-Eyed Pete.'

'Glass-Eyed Pete,' Billy repeated, and smiled. It was nice to clap a name and a face to the voice he'd heard in his dreams.

'Aye, lad, it's what they call me when I'm down on the docks or riding the waves.'

His ghostly green parrot squawked, not wanting to be left out.

'The bird's name is Jenkins. He's seen me round the world and a bit past it too. Followed me right into the Afterlife. Har. Well, now, what should we be calling ye? And where'd ye get the fine seagoing rigging?'

'Billy Bones is my name, sir. Dame Biglum just gave me these clothes.'

Billy would have bet a mountain of treasure that

all pirates were crafty scoundrels. He was surprised by this one's friendliness. *A pirate. A real pirate!*

'Sir? Such a polite fellow! And Dame Biglum? Which one? There's been five so far that I've known.'

'She mentioned that she was married to Sir Barkley Braggety Biglum the Fifth.'

'Maddy!'

Billy thought Dame Biglum was getting on in years. *But how could she have known him? She can't possibly be THAT old!*

'It's a happy horn blast. Glad to know she's still alive and kicking. I wasn't in that box as long as I feared.

'I'm thinking, my lad, yer due a reward for breaking me out. Open that sea chest. Ye will find something more than a little bit useful in there.'

Billy creaked the chest lid open. Inside was a fire-red vase. Next to it lay a small leather pouch and a golden medallion, which looked like a perfect lid for the vase. He picked up the medallion. A fierce-looking skull glared back at him. It looked quite crude and *very old*. The medallion was heavy for its size and tingled with energy.

As Billy held it, the gold disc brightened.

'It's ancient,' said Pete, 'and powerful as can be. Has a nasty effect on Afterlife magic, it does. "Existical energy" is what they call it. It's a kind of living magic, attached strongly to the Earth herself. The things in the trunk are filthy with the stuff. The magic in that medallion and that there vase is what trapped me.'

Pete rocked back and forth on his heels, elbows

out, thumbs tucked in his belt. He seemed delighted with his newfound freedom and eager to talk after being cooped up so tightly with only Jenkins for company.

'Millions of years ago, when the first livin' thing died, two magical energies were released. The two opposing energies grew in strength from that day to this. Eternal energy powers all the magic in the Afterlife, just like existical energy powers the magic in the living world.

'Neither energy can exist without the other. Lookin' at one helps ye understand the other, like black next to white, or ice and fire. Are ye catching me drift?'

'Yes, sir . . . existical energy and eternal energy,' Billy repeated, so Pete knew he'd been following along.

Pete nodded with a wispy grunt. 'It's a powerful secret I'm telling ye, boy. There's some in the Afterlife who'd be happy as a wind-filled sail to find this vase. The ones who would put it to their own foul use. They could suck up any unsuspecting spirit who got in their way. So I reckon ye and me should keep this to ourselves.'

Billy's blue eyes widened like saucers. Someone was trusting him with a secret! He swore to himself he'd hold it as tight as he could. Nervously he held the medallion out to the pirate. For a blink, it shimmered with rainbow colours.

Pete backed away. 'Don't bring that medallion too close, me boy. It won't do a ghost any good. That medallion could wreak havoc on the Afterlife itself. Full of power, ye see. Tuck it in the pouch, that's a lad.'

Billy leaned into the chest. Peeking out from the

leather pouch was Pete's real glass eye. Billy picked up the eye and bag, but as he did, he grazed the overturned vase.

'Heave to, boy!' Pete wailed as his whole body wavered towards the trunk like a wind-blown willow. Billy snapped his hands back, and Pete settled back into his ghostly form. 'That there vase is even more powerful than the rest. Don't be touching it again!'

Billy quickly tucked the glass eye and medallion into the faded leather bag and held it tight to his bony chest before he could do any more harm. 'Sorry, Mr Pete. I didn't know.'

'That's all right, me boy, I was just afraid I'd get sucked in again.' Pete floated towards Billy with a reassuring smile and patted him on the shoulder. 'Ye got to be careful around it, is all. Living people and skeletons can conduct existical energy, right through that vase. And the next thing ye know, a ghost like me is furled up inside. Now why don't ye show me that glass eye and I can tell ye all about it.'

CHAPTER 16

A CASE OF KIDNAPPING

A distant gong cut a lone note through the incense haze in the Temple of Maat. Miss Chippendale absentmindedly placed her jewel-encrusted goblet on the edge of a small table and waited for her guest. The forgotten cup wobbled and then pulled apart into nothingness.

Seconds later, two muscular servants opened the massive doors and two columns of temple guards carried in a golden litter. It looked like a fancy bed on poles, covered with a fabric roof. Reclining inside, the scarlet-robed figure of Gossip was quite obviously enjoying the company.

'Welcome, my dear. Why don't you join me up here? Care for a sip and a bite?' Miss Chippendale asked. She produced an additional throne and two goblets, a steaming pitcher of wine punch, elegant plates and a cheeseboard. Gossip accepted Miss Chippendale's gracious offer and snaked up to the

110

empty seat.

The manifestation daintily placed the plate in its serpentine lap while Miss Chippendale poured. It was unsettling to watch the apparition sipping hot wine.

'Ah, yesss, thank you. I should sssay, your drinks are as impressive as your household ssstaff.' Gossip cast a leering eyeball towards the retreating litter.

'Now, my friend,' said Miss Chippendale, 'about High Manners Manor and the goings on—'

'Bobbins and bells! There certainly are sssome peculiarities afoot . . . especially in the sssecrets closet. For years I've had a sssuspicion they kidnapped the sssoul of a missing boy.'

Miss Chippendale looked at Gossip with alarm. 'Why didn't you say something before now?'

'I would have, but it happened ssso very long ago. I've been in your ssservice for only a year.' Gossip saw the disappointment on Miss Chippendale's face and smoothly added, 'An arrangement I prize. I never imagined getting paid in golden wishes for sssnooping. If only I could spend those wishesss on Earth!'

'I can't imagine what interests you so much on Earth. It's a lowly place, filled with the living and skeletons.' Miss Chippendale stifled a burp.

'Oooh well, humans have sssuch delectable ssstories to share,' the manifestation continued. 'And who knows what other sssecrets those sssskeletons have in that closet. I'd give anything to have a look. Of course that's not the worst of it.' Gossip rolled out a self-satisfied smile.

'Don't keep it to yourself.' Miss Chippendale waited hungrily for more.

'It sseems an old friend of the Investigative Branch has popped up unexpectedly. Glass-Eyed Pete. I've heard Commissioner Pickerel is quite interested in him.'

The manifestation took a sip of the steaming punch. Cornelia Chippendale licked her lips and inched to the edge of her throne.

'Yes, it was quite a shock to sssee that nasty pirate again. He was hiding under our very noses. Delicious!'

Miss Chippendale's nod jiggled her chins.

'Now the young ssskeleton and the pirate appear to be in cahoots. Who knows what they're up to? It's time for a warrant to open that closet!'

'I'll have to see what Commissioner Pickerel says.' Miss Chippendale pursed her lips, then nibbled more cheese. 'Perhaps I should take it up with him now.'

Gossip sipped and demurely placed its goblet on the small table. 'Of course, my dear. I'd never want to get in the way of ssspreading news. And ssspeaking of news, I do wish you could share sssome with me, after all that I've shared with you.'

Miss Chippendale slyly revealed the latest goings-on in the department. Pickerel was steadily knocking off his last rivals in the Moral Authority and gaining complete control on the council. He had all but declared war on the skeletons over in the Hall of Reception and the Department of Fibs and Fabrications. Gossip swelled like a blowfish.

Finally Miss Chippendale set her goblet down. 'My servants will be happy to see you back to the manor.'

Miss Chippendale clapped her hands, and the servants escorted Gossip, all smiles, out of the throne room.

Miss Chippendale bounced off the dais like popcorn and ran towards the commissioner's office. She knew he'd be interested. Between accepting unacceptable goods, kidnapping and throwing their lot in with a rebel ghost, these skeletons were digging a deeper and deeper hole for themselves. Deep enough to warrant an investigation.

Within the hour, Commissioner Pickerel sent his best investigator: himself.

*　　　*　　　*

Mrs Bones had fretted all morning. The closet was too small to hold anything so disruptive as a snappish mood. Mr Bones heaved a sigh and watched her grumble over to straighten their sleeping trunk for the fifth time this morning. He spoke in his most loving voice. 'Plumkins, what do you say we open a few trunks and re-sort our favourite lies? That will keep us busy, eh?'

'Don't "Plumkins" me, Lars Bones. Our little Billy is somewhere out there!' Mrs Bones slammed the sleeping trunk lid. Dust billowed everywhere.

'What's out there is everything the boy has ever wished for, my dear. Besides, wasn't it your idea?'

'So now it's all my doing?' She clacked her hands on her hips. 'It's just as much your fault.'

Mr Bones ground his teeth into his pipe stem and took a deep breath. In two hundred years of marriage, he'd never seen her kick up such a fuss. 'Let's see how he is tonight.' Mr Bones hoped she would calm down when Billy checked in. He clicked his gold watch around in his finger bones

113

and thought the appointed hour couldn't come fast enough.

Mrs Bones stood stiffly by the sleeping trunk with her back to Mr Bones. A mist of tears wisped down her face and dripped on to the trunk. Mr Bones knocked a chair aside as he rushed to her side.

'Oh, Decette. Don't fret so.'

'I'm worried, Lars. I know he's not far away, but I miss him. What will we do if the Investigative Branch starts snooping around and we lose him altogether?'

'Let's not think about that unless we have to,' Mr Bones clucked.

A point of light emerged from the darkness, just centimetres away from Mr Bones's face. A special delivery cherub emerged from a circle of tinkling lights and dropped an envelope into his hands. The winged messenger twisted back into its baby-size portal and disappeared.

'A Hall of Reception seal . . . Must be important.' Mr Bones broke the seal and pulled out the enclosed letter. 'It's from Grim.'

Mr Bones fished for his spectacles and read the brief letter. Then he read it aloud. He wanted to read it a third time, but the letter and envelope burst into flames and vanished.

Mr Bones looked glumly at Mrs Bones. 'It's official. Now we should worry.'

CHAPTER 17

THE EYE

When Billy touched the glass eye, a remarkable thing happened. His vision split in two as he looked up at himself and down at his bony hand at the same time. Both views mixed together like a muddy puddle. He closed his own eyes and rotated the eye around so he could see different parts of the room. Scamp chirped and posed.

'It's a fine thing to have when yer sneaking around. Helps ye see around corners, it does,' explained the ancient pirate as he and Scamp looked over Billy's shoulder. 'And ye can see what's inside folks too.'

Billy kept his eyes closed and held the eyeball up to Pete. There was a misty swirl around the pirate's chest. Inside, Billy could make out two dragons locked in battle, one ghostly white, the other shadow black.

'Let me know what ye saw, Billy boy. I've always

had a powerful curiosity.'

Billy told him. 'Sounds about right,' the pirate nodded.

Billy turned the eye on himself. All he could see was his sailor shirt over an empty ribcage. 'How come I can't see inside myself?'

'Aye, that's a disappointment with the magic. Ye can see the stamp of another's soul, but not yer own. And be careful, boy, ye can't share that magic eye with anyone, ever, unless yer ready to give it up for good. So lash it to yerself tight.'

Billy popped the glass eye into the leather pouch and asked, 'What did it mean, those two dragons?'

The pirate's eyelids unfurled in concentration. 'It's a good question yer asking if yer going to be looking into another person's soul. I fear mine is twined with good and bad. Been a struggle with me, being a pirate and all, which is going to come out on top. So far, the good's been winning, and that's how I aim to keep it.'

The ghost walked towards the door. Pete could have glided horizontally as if reclining on a wind gust, but in the living world, he preferred to keep up with its mannerisms.

Billy closed the trunk with a heavy sigh.

The old ghost turned back to Billy and held his shoulder. 'Storm clouds are breaking over yer brows. What's wrong, lad?'

'Just wanted to know more about sailing six of the seven seas and running up a Jolly Roger, is all.' Billy couldn't bring himself to look the pirate in the eye. He didn't want the old salt to see the splash of his disappointment.

'Is that it, then? I'll tell ye what, Master Billy,

116

we'll find a more suitable port and I'll tell ye all the ins and outs of the pirate way. But first, maybe ye could steer me to my good friend Maddy?'

In answer, Billy skipped out in front to lead the way. Jenkins squawked and fluttered from Pete's shoulder as they left.

*   *   *

Soon Billy, Scamp and Pete arrived in the playroom. Billy showed Glass-Eyed Pete around.

'The place's just like I remember,' said Pete. He stood hands on hips, like he was in charge of his old pirate crew. 'Except for a bit of fading, it ain't changed a wink.'

Billy stood by the ancient sea dog and mimicked his pose.

'Ye look ready to be sailing the open sea, lad. Let's see ye kick up yer heels to this little jig.' The phantom pirate began to sing and bang a ghostly boot on the floor. As muffled as his ghostly shoe leather was, it still tattooed a fine rhythm.

Me an' ol' Marie
Set a course for the sea.
With a tin horn pipe
A dagger and a wife
We be happy as two birds can be.

The crew dreamed of matrimony
But no wives were found at sea
So they married a whale
And she sang like a gale
Every time they was late for tea.

Ohhhhhhh, 'tis a fine old life at sea
When you're a married man like me
With a tin horn pipe
And a dagger and a wife
We be happy as two birds can be.

Life was good as she could be
For that ol' whale, the crew, and Marie
Then the men went ashore
And the beer they did pour
'Til the whale chased 'em all back to sea . . .

By the third verse Billy and Glass-Eyed Pete had linked arms and were dancing in circles.

*   *   *

Dame Biglum and Millicent heard the ruckus in the next room. Millicent had already completed her tea bag sewing and returned to the attic. The two of them peeked into the playroom. Millicent was openmouthed at the sight, but Dame Biglum's smile almost burst its seams seeing Glass-Eyed Pete singing and dancing with Billy. 'Wherever you've been all these years, Greatest Grandfather Biglum, you haven't lost a step.'

Pete turned and smiled. 'There ye be, my greatest granddaughter-in-law! And who is this darling lass?'

'That would be your great-great . . . urm . . . great-many-greats granddaughter.' Dame Biglum motioned Millicent forward. Millicent made a wide-eyed curtsy and the pirate's face broke into a creaky grin. He drifted over for a gentle (although

118

cold) hug.

He hugged Dame Biglum too. 'I've missed ye, Maddy, but I've been a lot closer than ye think. Billy here just sprang me from the trap one of yer twins set for me. A good many years ago, eh, Jenkins?' The parrot ruffled his feathers and looked sceptically through his un-patched eye. 'I don't suppose they'd be around so I could give them a piece of my mind, would they?'

Dame Biglum clouded up.

The pirate stepped back to study his old friend. 'Oh, now I've put my ghostly foot in it. What's the matter, girlie? What have I said?'

Dame Biglum once again told the story of the missing Goodwin and how Sir Barkley Braggety Biglum VI had grown into a more monstrous man than her husband, The Fifth.

'Sorry to hear it, Maddy. Sounds like yer times have been even harder than mine. This manor needs a good turn on the wheel—it's high past time we straightened her course. What do ye say, lad?'

Of course, anything that sounded at all like pirating met with Billy's approval.

Dame Biglum, on the other hand, was more reserved. 'I don't know . . . I prefer to leave my son and that dreadful housekeeper alone. They're rotten to the bone.'

'Oh, I see they've laid into ye pretty good over the years. Tell ye what, ye can give them a piece of yer mind when yer feeling up to it. Until then, Billy and me will sort things out.'

'Don't forget about me!' Millicent cried, stepping forward.

'It's a fine thing to have another set of hands for

the rigging!' Pete's grin grew almost larger than his face could carry. 'Good to know there's another true heart born into this cursed family. There've been so many bad ones.' The pirate wrapped a hand around his stubbly chin. 'Hope yer plenty cagey and wily too. Ye'll need all that to square off against this family.'

Billy stepped next to Millicent like a sailor waiting for orders.

Pete nodded, 'Aye, ye look ready as can be. Now why don't ye give me a few minutes with Maddy here so we can catch up, eh?'

Everyone made themselves comfortable back in Dame Biglum's room. As the grown-ups chatted, Billy and Millicent whispered quietly together on the sofa. Billy excitedly told her all about the secret stairwell in the playroom, and how he had found Glass-Eyed Pete trapped in the basement.

He'd tried his best to keep mum about the vase and medallion, but the secret slid out. Millicent promised she would keep the secret and do her best to help Billy keep quiet as well. Although she wished the vase could suck Miss Primly inside as easily as a ghost.

While Billy was recounting the rest of his adventures, Millicent kept glancing at the chest of drawers. Finally, Billy stopped and said, 'I'd think pirates, hidden passageways and magic would get your attention. What's the matter?'

'There's something about that picture . . . It was eating at me earlier. Let's have a proper look at it.'

Millicent led Billy to the chest of drawers and picked up one of the portraits. She held it beside Billy's head. She looked from the picture to the face and the face to the picture. 'There's something about the eyes . . .'

She turned the picture towards Billy, and he went paler than one would have thought possible for a skeleton.

'I've seen that boy before. He was the boy in the closet . . . I think he was *me*!'

'Exactly. I guess your mum and dad would even say so.' Millicent wanted to raise the picture over her head and run all the way to the secrets closet shouting, 'See? See? See?' Instead, she clutched it to her chest like a book she'd just finished, one solving a particularly satisfying mystery.

'Don't bet too much. They're close-mouthed with a secret.'

'Well, Billy Bones, I think we should feel proud for answering an important part of this riddle,' Millicent smiled.

They decided to probe Mr and Mrs Bones later on. In the meantime, they spent the rest of very a pleasant afternoon in the playroom.

*   *   *

That evening, Martha brought a plentiful supper to Dame Biglum. With such generous portions, Millicent could tuck in as well. Billy spent more time in the wardrobe, but Pete didn't have to hide. Martha couldn't see ghosts, or other things that ought not to be there.

After dinner was cleared away, Dame Biglum was tired. Pete escorted Billy and Millicent to her attic room. The two little figures chattered and skipped with childlike energy, but Pete was growing more transparent by the hour.

The three settled into Millicent's room. Glass-

Eyed Pete was good as his word to Billy and spun a yarn about his old pirating days.

'Billy and Millicent, I have to confess to ye there was a time me heart was as slippery as a snake's shadow. But none of us was as mean as me very first captain: Half-Faced Nelson. His ship was known as the Spurious, and she was hard and cruel to any who crossed her wake.

'Half-Faced Nelson had a meeting with a cannonball and came out on the sorry end of the introductions. It twisted him into one cruel pirate, sure enough. Ye'd want a shark for a nursemaid before ye'd ever want to dock next to him.

'One moonless night, we was tracking a Spanish galleon. Half-Face sent all aboard the ship to swim with the fishes. Aye, it's a terrible fact, Billy and Millicent, but Half-Face's heart was smaller than a peppercorn.

'We took a mountain of treasure from the Spanish lady. Half-Face kept most of it, but he tossed a few trinkets to the crew. He didn't know what he was giving up when he tossed me the glass eye, red vase and matching golden medallion, and a couple of other powerful relics. Full of magic they were, and still are today.

'I didn't understand the wonder of what I had right away, I just thought the eye might improve me appearance a mite. After years of capturing treasure and tucking it into chests, I started looking closer at the sea dogs I was shipping with. It was a disgusting sight. So I tried to mend me ways.

'That's when I built the manor yer standing in now—at least the bare bones of it (begging yer pardon there, Billy). A lot's been added over the

122

years. And it vexes me no end to see how it's become the pompous piece of work that ye see today.'

Pete finished his tale with a stamp of his boot. Then he winced and faded even more.

'Are you all right, Mister Pete?' Billy called.

'Aye, Master Billy. Don't be fretting yerself.' Pete took his hat off and rubbed his face with a withered hand, then showed them a thin smile. 'Children, me and Jenkins got to go for a while. This here world is draining us dry. Takes a special effort for ghosts to spend time on Earth, ye see. We need to rest up for a bit in the Afterlife.'

'You're not going for long, I hope!' Billy clattered over to the ghost's fading form.

'Not on yer life,' Glass-Eyed Pete chuckled. He gathered the children in for the last hug of the night, and shimmered off to heaven knows where (or maybe it doesn't).

CHAPTER 18

MIDNIGHT ESCAPE

When night arrived at the doorstep of the mansion, the clocks rang out the hour. It reminded the children that another mountain of dishes was waiting in the scullery. Billy took the hidden staircase, while Millicent used the servants' stairwell.

She ran into Gossip skulking near the third-floor landing.

'Oooh, the little girl with the sssenile grandmother,' Gossip hissed, sliding close.

Gossip's breath washed over Millicent. It smelt of swamp water and stinking half-truths. Millicent turned her head away in disgust. 'She is not crazy!'

Gossip smirked and slithered around to face Millicent again. 'That'sss not what I hear. Cuckoo as a four-handed clock, everyone sssays. Even her daughter ran away from the crazy old loon.' The manifestation poked Millicent's chest. Its curved finger was surprisingly hard. 'Not much of a daughter, was she?'

Millicent's eyes welled up. The manifestation's foul-smelling mouth was only centimetres away as it whispered, 'And now she's too busy to visit you.'

'She's visits all the time!'

'But where is she now? It's been quite a while sssince she dropped by.' Gossip began to snake away, then turned and added, 'Make sssure you tell me if she ever shows up, and that uncaring father of yours too. I have grave doubts they will.'

Millicent screamed, 'THEY WILL!'

But the scarlet glow of the manifestation disappeared down the hall, laughter echoing behind.

'You great big LIAR!' Millicent shouted. Then she bit her lip.

Millicent didn't have much time to sulk. Brisk footsteps were coming her way. She dashed out of the servants' stairwell, into an elegant hallway, and behind a suit of armour.

Miss Primly swooshed by. Her sharp features poked out from the soft lace of her night bonnet.

She stopped next to the armour and looked around. Suspicion twisted her face. She muttered a string of curses, ending with, 'When I find out who's making this ruckus, I'll stuff their shouts down their throats. And if they've wakened the master, I'll jump in too with both legs!'

Millicent held her breath until the old scourge moved on. Down the hallway, Miss Primly slowed and trod with more care. She stopped short and peered into the front hallway. She paused and listened . . . Silence. Even the manor's typical groans seemed curious.

Primly stretched forward and listened once more, and then stormed back upstairs—grumbling every *snick-snacking* step of the way.

Millicent knew she was due in the kitchen. But she just had to find out what was around the corner. After making sure no housekeepers or manifestations lurked, she inched forward into another hallway.

Halfway down the expanse of marble and palms, Millicent spotted an opened door. A haze of cigar smoke drifted into the hallway. She tiptoed forward from palm to palm.

Peeping around the doorframe, she saw a luxurious living room and a doorway to another large room. The second room held several tall chests of drawers and an emperor-sized bed. Both rooms were painted a rich emerald green. The living room was dark except for a lamp burning on a table next to a reading chair. Its back faced Millicent. A man's arm in a crimson silk dressing gown rested on the chair's thick green padding. His snores sounded like a clockwork toy being wound and unwound.

Over the fireplace, Millicent noticed a painting that covered nearly the whole wall. The man in the portrait was bulky and bald. Eyes the size of Millicent's head glared into the dark room. In one fist he grasped the lapel of his black velvet coat. The ring finger bore a large gold signet ring embossed with the Biglum crest. It matched the hand on the chair's occupant.

This was Sir Biglum's room.

Millicent heard footsteps tapping towards her. She slid behind a fern next to the doorway and waited.

It was Higgins, Sir Biglum's butler. He knocked on the door. 'Sir, the gentleman from Hack, Whack and Plunder will soon arrive.'

'BLAST, it, man! You gave me a start,' Sir Biglum's voice boomed out. 'A fellow can't close his eyes for more than a minute without some rude interruption. I'll BOIL the next servant who disturbs me!'

Higgins remained unruffled. 'Beg your pardon, sir, but the lawyer? Where would you like me to take him?'

'To a SIBERIAN sinkhole, for all the good he's done lately,' Sir Biglum grumbled. 'When he arrives, show him to my study. I'll be down in a moment.'

Higgins bowed like a well-greased hinge and left. As the echoes of his footsteps retreated, Millicent huddled behind the ceramic planter and for a lonely moment she thought of her parents.

Then the gears in the hall clock whirred and belted out the quarter hour. She was late! Millicent scampered down to the kitchen for her last night in the scullery.

Cook was waiting in a wobbly state. She had been emptying bottles again. She banged her wooden spoon woozily and growled at Millicent to get busy.

Once again, the job went much quicker with Billy's help. He had emerged from the cupboard under the stairs and the two of them scaled the mountain of dishes together. They soaped, rinsed, sorted and stacked with the same quiet efficiency of Billy's skeleton parents filing secrets in their closet.

*   *   *

Millicent's hands were still damp when they arrived at the closet. Mr and Mrs Bones were overjoyed to see Billy. They gripped him and Millicent in bone-crunching hugs and asked all about the day. Billy excitedly told them.

Then, being such a horrid secrets keeper, Billy spouted, 'Mum and Dad, Millicent and I think we've puzzled a few pieces together about Dame Biglum's missing son, Goodwin.'

Like the truth, thought Millicent. She skipped to a trunk and took a seat. As she sat with the skeleton family, she drew in their warmth as if she was reading by the fireside.

'Billy, you know we can't discuss other people's secrets,' cautioned Mr Bones.

'Mr Bones,' Millicent piped in, 'couldn't you at least tell us if we're right or wrong?'

The skeleton set his jaw. 'It would be against all my professional ethics, my dear.'

'Then I guess we'll have to figure this out for ourselves.' Millicent winked at Billy.

Billy stifled a smile. 'Dad, you can tell us about it. You told me about my adoption.'

'My boy, that was our secret.' Mr Bones turned to his wife, switching subjects before the children could press further. 'The world outside seems good for our Billy, dear. Shall we give him a few more days with Millicent?'

'Lars, I'm not sure . . .'

'The boy needs to stretch his leg bones. He's living a skeleton's dream out there. Who could imagine our own Billy enjoying that kind of freedom?' Mr Bones leaned close to Mrs Bones and whispered, 'Besides, we need to talk . . .'

Mrs Bones wrung her hands. 'All right then, off with you two. But promise me—'

'I know, I won't let any humans see me,' Billy assured her.

After a weepy hug from Mrs Bones, the pair were off, giggling quietly as they closed the secrets-closet door and stood in the dark passageway.

Normally at this late hour, Millicent would be fighting off sleep. But not tonight. She was thinking about something too exciting. She leaned close to Billy and whispered, 'I think it's time we break out of this prison and have a real explore!'

'Outside?' Billy gasped.

'Yes, you dilly. And right away!'

'But how?'

Millicent's enthusiasm dimmed as she and Billy wondered how to make their escape without being seen.

Billy stuck his hands in the sailor suit pockets. His fingers met the leather pouch and his smile widened. He pulled out the glass eye and showed it to Millicent. 'It's just the thing for seeing around corners.'

'Let me try it.'

But she was disappointed when the eye just rolled around in her palm.

'It only works for the owner,' Billy couldn't help a small gloat, 'unless the owner decides to give it up for good. That won't be happening soon, I can tell you.'

She handed it back with a small smile. 'Good to know we have a little magic on our side.' Just as they turned to sneak towards the kitchen, purple light glowcd ahead.

'Quick, hide in the shadows. Someone's coming!' Billy hissed. Millicent slipped around the corner and waited.

A hole opened up in the air, a skeleton's hand brushed aside an airy curtain, and out hobbled Mr Benders. He limped towards Billy, grimacing with every step.

'Thundering thumb bones, lad! What are you doing out of the closet?' But before Billy could answer, Mr Benders stumbled and winced. 'Arrrrr . . . This hip's hurting something awful . . .' He fished a letter from his bag. 'Could you get this to your parents, lad? It's straight from the Hall of Reception. And give them my regards as well.'

The letter seemed to come alive as it shook in Billy's hands. *Must be a secret,* he thought. He looked for an official marking, but the envelope was blank.

Just before Mr Benders disappeared to the Afterlife, he turned to Billy and added, 'I see what you're up to. You're mighty considerate to give your folks a little privacy. Keeps the marriage knots tied firm and tight.'

The glowing hole closed, and Mr Benders was gone.

Millicent sneaked back around the corner. She took one look at Billy and burst out laughing.

'Yes . . . um . . .' Billy said. 'I'd better give them the letter. I think there's a secret inside.'

'Oh Billy,' Millicent pouted, 'we were just about to break out of here. Why don't you give it to them later? Besides—' Millicent clutched her hands to her heart and fluttered her eyelashes—'they could be snuggling!'

Billy rolled his eyes. 'OK. Let's go.'

He promised himself to get the letter into his parents' hands as soon as he returned. He shoved it into his pocket, and they made for the servants' entrance. Unfortunately, the way was through the kitchen: they would have to get by Cook again.

The kitchen door stood open. Billy tucked the eye around the doorframe. Cook was flopped over the table. Dribble pooled next to her open mouth. He rotated the eye around to make sure no one else was in the room. As he swivelled the eye past Cook, a globby green eyestalk emerged from her back and looked around.

Seeing Cook's ugly soul, Billy almost dropped the magic eye. But he held on and slipped it back into the leather bag. They tiptoed past Cook and soon passed through the narrow servants' entrance and out of the manor.

It was a splendid night. Billy plunked himself down in the grass and ran his bony palm over the thick blades in wonder while Millicent danced across the west lawn and spun till she toppled over.

As she waited for her vision to stop spinning, she noticed a light on in Sir Biglum's ground-floor study.

Coaxing Billy to the study was slow work. He wanted to stop and examine every twig, leaf and tiny bug. He was especially interested in two rabbits that dashed into their warren when he approached.

'Billy!' Millicent whispered bossily. 'If you don't keep up with me, we'll just have to go back inside!'

'Hold on to your undies. You've been outside before, but I never have,' Billy whispered back.

The two explorers circled towards the study, pressing close to the juniper hedges. A raised

131

porch jutted out. The children hid behind its rail posts and peered straight into an open window.

Sir Biglum was talking to a weaselly man hidden in a black overcoat with velvet trim. They could only see the top of his oily hair over his upturned collar. Judging by the scowl on Sir Biglum's face, the meeting wasn't going well.

'The men who brought me here on the train wore coats like that. We need to get closer,' whispered Millicent.

Billy was thrilled by her daring. It's what a pirate would do, he reminded himself. But if he'd had a stomach it would have flipped. The two crept up the porch steps to the window.

CHAPTER 19

A SHADOWY ENCOUNTER

A sharp wind sliced through the neighbouring field. Grim's towering horse stopped on the grounds of High Manners Manor. Grim dropped from Fleggs's saddle, his riding boots denting the perfect lawn.

The whispers in the halls of the Righteousness Department were multiplying by the hour. There would certainly be an investigation. And when they looked into Lars Bones's small misstep, they were going to find Grim's more extravagant one. He had to cover his tracks. Something must be done about the boy.

The more he thought about it, the more he was convinced this was the proper course. The boy could be trained in the Afterlife. Perhaps he'd become an exceptional secrets keeper, just like his foster parents. Lars and Decette might even thank Grim one day. Yes, it was practically his *duty* to put things back to rights: secrets belonged in secrets closets, and illegal skeleton nephews belonged in the Afterlife.

Lucky thing he'd persuaded Cecil Benders to deliver the letter, with the secret document tucked inside. Relying on the Afterlife's regular post risked prying eyes. Still, he felt uncomfortable using Benders like that.

Over the last fifty years, Grim's strict professionalism had kept him from forming attachments to many souls. But Billy was another matter. His brother and sister-in-law had wanted a son so badly. While many miraculous things happen in the Afterlife, having children isn't one of them. This is only for the living—and a sad fact for Lars and Decette with so much love to share. They'd pined for a child since the day they married.

Grim had been careless with the rules of the Afterlife. He had bent them, perhaps past the breaking point, for Lars and Decette. But now Grim had to act to save his skin (or lack of it) and Lars's and Decette's as well. If the High Council found them guilty, they'd be given a one-way ticket to Nevermore, sure as death follows life.

Grim shivered. It was time to send the boy over to the other side—past time, really.

He wrapped himself tightly in the cloak of doom and strode towards the manor.

*   *   *

Billy and Millicent peeked around the edge of the open window. Sir Biglum was scolding the representative from Hack, Whack and Plunder.

'Mr Whack, I was counting on your firm, but your people BUNGLED the job! I don't care if you have to turn every one of my tenants out on the street. I said TRIPLE their rent!'

'Then we'll have to fix up the apartments to attract more suitable tenants, sir.' The man rubbed his large palms together as if he was lathering soft soap. 'A brilliant business mind such as yours knows that could get quite expensive.'

'BAH! Just raise the rents and be done with it. I need the money NOW!' Sir Biglum's face matched his crimson dressing gown.

'As you wish.' The man shifted in his chair and leaned forward. 'There is some good news on your other inquiry though. You were right: Artemis Hues was worth a fortune. He was considered some kind of genius in the art world. We found one of his paintings. It's worth a very pretty penny.' The man's hands were expressive as puppets when he rubbed his thumb back and forth across his fingertips. 'The gallery owner, some Frenchman by the name of Monsieur Henri Bouche De Sourire, said he was looking for Hues's other paintings too. They've gone missing.'

Millicent edged closer for a better look. Billy tried to pull her back, but she shrugged him off. He was going to try again when he heard something shuffle through the grass. *Probably one of the little bunnies,* he thought.

The next sound was a chair leg scraping across floorboards inside. Billy tucked in next to Millicent and listened.

'RIGHT!' Sir Biglum smirked. 'This *is* good news. I want your firm to draw up papers immediately. That painting. That delightfully

135

expensive and invaluable painting belongs to my niece. We must have it IMMEDIATELY.'

'For your niece?'

'Are you DAFT? For the PRESTIGE it will add to my bi-quadrennial ball. And second . . . for the MONEY! I want that painting! Then I want you to search high and low for the others.'

'Perhaps we should speak to your niece? A little aggressive questioning could tumble a clue or two.' The man balled his hands into fists.

'Excellent suggestion. It's something I'd enjoy doing myself. And soon, I suspect. Now, Mr Whack, this meeting is OVER!'

Millicent and Billy heard shuffling as the men departed.

Something stirred just beyond the porch. Billy leaned over the railing, then jumped back, horrified, clutching at the ivy.

'Hector's spectre!' cried Billy.

But Millicent was too furious to notice. 'Did you hear?' she asked. 'He's going to steal my father's painting!'

Tossing a last look back at the window, Millicent marched to the steps.

Billy pressed closer to the wall. 'Millicent, wait . . .'

Millicent blinked back tears as she thumped down the stairs and right into the hot breath of two growling bullmastiffs.

She froze.

Billy's knees knocked like drumsticks. *Some pirate you're going to be,* he scolded himself.

The huge dogs inched closer. The fur on their scruffs was raised in a warning, haunches tensed to leap. But Billy struck first. He landed in front of

Millicent, ready to take on all comers. 'Back off! Let the lady pass!'

Most dogs, presented with such a delicious assortment of bones, would have tucked in and gnawed contentedly. Instead, they yelped and ran off into the darkness.

Millicent let out a deep breath and touched Billy's shoulder. 'That was really brave, Billy. Thank you.'

The young skeleton was nearly as surprised as the dogs. He relaxed and grinned at his friend. 'I guess I'm scarier than I thought!'

*   *   *

Uncle Grim smiled to himself from the darkness of the nearby hedges. *Thank goodness Billy's not in the secrets closet. It would have been dreadful dealing with him while Lars and Decette watched.*

He chuckled quietly as he watched Billy's antics on the steps. *Looks like the seed of piracy is still sprouting in those Biglums. It's a shame I have to ship this one off.*

Of course it was Grim who had panicked the dogs. A simple rustling of his cloak had sent the smell of death and destruction into their sensitive noses.

Grim rolled up his sleeves. Normally, one swipe of his scythe's curved blade would have been enough to cut anyone's mortal thread. Then with a dark, sparkling pinch of eternal energy, he'd transport the soul to the Afterlife. But Billy was already dead. Grim had cut his thread twenty-five years before. Since then, Billy's soul had become quite accustomed to the Earth. Grim was sure he'd have to use quite a jolt of eternal energy to accomplish his task. He stole forward through the bushes, as close as he dared, and removed his gloves.

One by one each glowing fingertip shimmered in black pinpoints of crackling energy. Slowly Grim turned to face Billy and raised his bony hands.

Grim prepared to stop time and yank Billy's soul into the Afterlife.

*   *   *

'We should be getting back inside,' Millicent reminded Billy.

Billy nodded and dumped the contents of his leather pouch into his hand. The glass eye bumped against the magic medallion. He was about to put the medallion back in the bag when the envelope in his pocket grew hot. It felt like it was going to burst into flames.

The letter! He struggled to grab it from his pocket, but it flew away towards the hedge. *No!* The Oculus exploded out of nowhere, and the light of truth lit up the hedge. Billy spotted a shadow in the shrubs fleeing the scene. The moonlight caught a glint of bone. Then the secret exploded, and Billy and Millicent were thrown back on the grass.

Millicent didn't stir, but Billy scrambled back to his feet as a vision unfolded.

He could see both his skeleton parents swaying in obvious despair. *Whose eyes am I looking through?* Billy wondered. Mr Bones, Mrs Bones and a stranger watched over the boy Billy had last seen in the portrait on Dame Biglum's chest of drawers. The boy looked like he was wasting away.

He must have been in the closet for weeks without food and water. Mr and Mrs Bones pleaded with the stranger. 'He's in too much pain!' Mrs Bones sobbed.

'Can you change him into a skeleton?' Mr Bones asked. 'He's not getting a proper burial, so he'll be a skeleton in the Afterlife, as it is. And then maybe . . . he could stay with us?'

'It means a trip for us all to a dark hole in Nevermore if anyone finds out,' the stranger's voice warned.

'Surely they'd understand. He's going to die anyway.' Mrs Bones pleaded.

Dark sparks of eternal energy washed round the child and winked away, revealing a skeleton. He lay there like a fallen headstone. After a long moment, he cried out and moved. Mrs Bones wept as she hugged the little skeleton boy.

'Thank you. We'll never tell a soul,' Mr Bones promised the stranger.

As the vision faded, Billy noticed the lawn had grown quiet, save for the wind shuffling through the hedge leaves. Millicent sat on the ground behind him, unmoving. Then the leaves froze and, like a dropped clock, time stood still.

An instant later, a dazzling light split the air next to him. Billy felt himself being pulled from his bones. He looked back to see a skeleton boy in a sailor suit standing in a state of shock.

The skeleton wobbled on its feet, then exploding with rainbow colours, it snatched Billy's glowing soul and pulled back. But, at the same time, a black stream of eternal energy twined around the bony hands and tried to yank Billy's soul into the bushes.

139

For a few amazing minutes the two opposing magics, existical and eternal, were locked in a battle of life and death.

Billy clamped his eyes shut. Something snapped and he was rocked back as the two magics poured into his body. It felt like a switch had been thrown between two thunderbolts. He shrieked. His marrow bubbled, lava hot. From his toes to his eyeballs, Billy felt like he'd been ripped inside out.

The glowing portal to the Afterlife closed.

Time started again.

Billy staggered drunkenly, feeling an unusual weight dragging him down. He stared at his hands in amazement. As the final flickers of colour washed away, he saw the hands of a chubby, live, flesh-and-blood boy.

*   *   *

Grim stared in horror at his own hands as the dark sparks blinked out. He felt weak, as if he'd been drained of power. Which meant his previous troubles had been a trifle until now. Grim could stop time, cut mortal coils, and travel easily between the two worlds. If he had accidentally transferred some of that magic to a living boy, he couldn't imagine what the High Council would have to say about it.

Then he heard something that really jangled his nerves—a voice all too familiar on both sides of existence.

'Ooooh, what do we have here?' Gossip's scarlet form wisped passed Billy. 'Hmm. People in high placesss are going to want to know about thisss,' the manifestation purred, and twisted off to spread

140

more maliciousness.

Grim pulled his cloak tighter and counted his blessings that Gossip hadn't seen him. He melted away into the bushes and back to Fleggs.

* * *

Millicent's head felt like it had been stuffed with cotton. She got up slowly.

A boy was weaving towards her. The boy from the picture! And he was wearing the same sailor suit Billy had had on just moments before.

He staggered to the steps, 'Look 'er me,' he mumbled and sat down heavily.

Millicent squinted, then blinked. She shook her head a few times, muttering, 'This *is* a peculiar house!' Finally looking up, she said, 'Well, Billy, not that I doubted myself for a second, but looking at you now, even Mr Bones will have to admit you're the long-lost Goodwin.'

Billy pinched himself a few times. He wasn't dreaming. He was sitting in the body of a stout ten-year-old boy. Billy couldn't help but pinch and poke every part of this new suit of flesh and blood.

Millicent brightened a moment later. 'But now we have a new mystery to solve. What in the world just happened to you, and how?'

It was time to get back. She guided Billy and carefully squeaked the back door open. Thankfully, Cook was still snoring. They made it up to the attic—and to a whole host of new challenges, now that Billy was a living, breathing and, at the moment, very tired boy.

Part 2

LIVING IN LIGHT

In darkness you can choose to live
But in light a truer life will give.
This fact of light is ever true
It always catches up to you.

Some advice, you should abide
Do not use the dark to hide.
Rather, use the dark for rest
And never put the truth to test.

CHAPTER 20

WELCOME HOME

Fitful.

The word didn't go anywhere near to describing Billy's night. He'd spent it in Millicent's trunk, popping awake any number of times—sometimes because an arm or a leg was tingling from lack of circulation, and other times in a sweat, convinced someone was yanking his soul out of his body.

Then there was the strange dream. At least, he was pretty sure it had been a dream.

He remembered sitting up in the trunk, but finding himself in an entirely different elsewhere filled with clouds and sky. Strangest of all, he was back in his skeleton body. He examined his arms—they glowed blue and flashed dark sparks of eternal energy—the same glow and sparks that surrounded Uncle Grim.

But the odd dream and tingling body bits weren't the only thing keeping him awake. His

145

sleepless brain crawled with questions.

How would his parents react to seeing him alive? What about the envelope with the secret inside? What kind of trouble was he in for losing it? Billy was pretty sure Mr Benders would never trust him again. What if Mr and Mrs Bones followed suit and lock the secrets closet on him for good?

At least Scamp had accepted him. Billy wondered how his chum recognized him so quickly. But Scamp explained that hardly anyone speaks Bug, so he'd picked out Billy's peculiar accent straight away.

He rubbed his face with his hands, feeling the smooth new layers of skin. He studied his hands in the dim light, then remembered the vision's hand: the glossy leather glove sticking out of a midnight-black sleeve. Was it Uncle Grim who had touched his mother's shoulder? Who else had the power to take a soul? Billy's cheeks flushed for the first time in many years. How could he even think of blaming his heroic uncle?

The questions swarmed like fire ants until morning's first light. Then Billy stuffed all his fidgety confusions into a lingering sigh and tried for a few more minutes' sleep.

*   *   *

Dame Biglum had seen some strange things over the years. For the better part of her adult life she had been fast friends with a ghost, had often battled Despair, and most recently befriended a skeleton boy.

Even all that experience with the unnatural side

146

of things couldn't prepare her for the sight of her own long-lost son standing before her. A jumble of joy and regret for time lost exploded in her heart. 'Goodwin!' It was all she could say as she swept the boy into her arms.

Billy was happy for the hug, but still deeply confused. To go from new acquaintance to long-lost son in one day is a lot to absorb for a boy of ten (even one who had been ten for the last twenty-five years).

Sensing his uncertainty, the old woman released him and leaned back on her cane.

'I'm sorry, my dears, for being so teary, but you'll have to help an old fuddy-duddy piece this together.' She dabbed her cheeks with her handkerchief.

Millicent and Billy explained as much as they could about the transformation—which was not much. Millicent knew there'd been a tremendous explosion and somehow Billy had turned into a living boy. Billy struggled to tell Dame Biglum about the tug of war on his soul. But the memory was too painful to describe.

However, he had plenty to say about the secrets closet: how someone had dumped him there years before, and how the Boneses had taken such good care of him over all that time.

'They sound like a lovely couple, my boy,' Dame Biglum said. 'It would be a privilege to meet them. Do you suppose they might drop by for a visit?'

'Oh, no. They can't come here,' Billy answered quickly. 'They have to guard the secrets.'

'Secrets, yes, we certainly have a few of them here at the manor.' Dame Biglum nodded sadly.

'I should say. They're stacked to the rafters

down there.' Billy told her about his parents' work down in the closet—the collecting, sorting, guarding, even the terrible explosions and strange visions when secrets are exposed.

'It sounds like they have a frightfully important job, Billy. They must be a wonderful couple. I'd dearly love to meet them someday. Hopefully while I'm still on this side of the living.' Dame Biglum stroked Billy's mop of brown hair. 'Now, why don't we have Martha bring us up some breakfast? You must be starving, my love. You haven't eaten for years.'

Dame Biglum called down to the kitchen, and Martha was soon up with a tray. Billy hid in the wardrobe. The smell of the food loosed a hunger in him, like a lion roar rattling dishes. When Martha left, he laid into the eggs, toast and tea. Dame Biglum had to caution him to slow down, for fear he'd choke.

After a few hours' visit, much of it spent reviewing proper table manners, Dame Biglum rapped a spoon on her drinking glass and addressed the children. 'I've decided I mustn't be greedy, Billy. I'm sure your skeleton parents will be anxious to see what's become of you. Perhaps you should call on them. I wish I had it in me to join you, children. But I'm afraid there are some below I am not willing to face. Not yet . . .'

She hugged Billy once more. He blinked back at her with the same soft blue eyes he had had as a skeleton. Dame Biglum wondered why she hadn't recognized him at once. She tousled his hair and smiled gently. 'I don't know how this can be, but I'm so glad you've come back, Goodwin. I never want to lose you again. It would be entirely too

148

much to bear.'

Billy was still confused by the strange goings-on, but he was clear on one thing. 'Could you stick with Billy? I'm not so sure about that Goodwin name.'

Dame Biglum saw his discomfort. 'Very well then, dear boy. Billy it is.'

*   *   *

Millicent and Billy stood in front of the secrets closet. It had been a long trip for Billy. He was still getting used to his new body. It wasn't nearly as airy as his skeleton bones, and he'd worked up a pretty good sweat. Millicent held an oil lamp up to the hanging key and spoke a truth. 'Sir Biglum is a thief!' This time the key was quicker to open the door, as this was a more significant truth.

Mr Bones spied Millicent from the back of the closet and darted towards her, eyes wide. 'Millicent! Thank goodness! What happened last night? We've been in a horrible panic. These trunks were rumbling like an elephant's carriage on cobblestones. Especially the ones with our secrets.'

Then the object of his worry walked in, and Mr Bones dropped his pipe. 'Billy! My boy! How did . . . ? What in the world . . . ?' A smile rubbed around his face like a hungry cat as he wrapped Billy in a fatherly hug. 'Decette, come at once!'

Mrs Bones click clacked over while Mr Bones picked up his pipe. 'Billy! Oh, Billy! We were so worried!'

'The way these trunks were jumping, we feared the worst. But look at you! Fresh and fine as the day we first met,' Mr Bones clucked, giving Mrs Bones a turn with the boy.

At first Mrs Bones could only stare, hands clasped to her chest. Then she grabbed Billy and danced around him with a girlishness that should have been exhausted centuries before. Her eyes glistened with foggy tears of joy. Billy was near tears himself, so relieved the door hadn't been slammed in his face.

But a knot of guilt tightened in his stomach. He'd lost the letter. They were happy to see him now, but what if they knew he'd lost an irreplaceable document? The secret clawed inside him, trying to get out, but he pushed it down. It was shamefully clear he couldn't be trusted with anything important. *And what about Nevermore? Mum and Dad could be in real danger all because of me.* He shivered at the thought of that dark and solitary doom.

Mr Bones clapped Billy on the back. 'Now tell us what happened.'

Billy mustered a small smile. 'I'm not sure. I just know one minute someone tried to pull me out of my body and the next, I was a real boy. He nearly added: *And I think it was Uncle Grim.* But he still couldn't believe his uncle was guilty. Grim was Billy's idol.

Millicent jumped in. 'I wonder if it was that red glow-y thing I saw there. Grandmother Maddy calls them manifestations.'

'Gossip?' Mr and Mrs Bones traded worried looks.

'He tried to cover his tracks, and now everyone will know.' Mrs Bones clapped her hand bones to her mouth.

150

'Decette,' Mr Bones snapped, 'hold your tongue.'

'So it was someone else?' Millicent asked with a glimmer of hope the skeletons would tell, just this once.

Mrs Bones looked at Mr Bones with a pleading look, but he shook his head. 'You know that's a secret we can't discuss. I can only say this much: we are under suspicion for irregularities in our service to the DFF. Now, that's all I'll tell you. The last thing we need is more irregularity here.'

He jammed his pipe in his mouth, patted Billy on the shoulder, and sighed. 'I must say, I'm a bit jealous, my boy. Now you can go anywhere . . . anywhere in the whole world . . .'

Billy was now thinking the unthinkable. Mrs Bones's slip convinced him it was Grim, for sure.

Mrs Bones drew Billy close and glared at Mr Bones. 'Even though your father doesn't agree, you're family, and I think we owe you some rather important truths!'

'Decette. That's where we got in trouble in the first place, by letting family come before duty!'

'Oh, so you think it was a mistake to have asked him for a son?'

'That's not what I said.'

'It most certainly was!'

The bony parents began to quarrel. Billy tried to tell them that he knew the truth, but Mr Bones interrupted him. 'Perhaps you children should come back in a little while.'

Billy closed the door behind him sadly. The click of the lock was like a starter's gun, sending the Bones's muffled argument back off to the races.

CHAPTER 21

LUNCH IS SERVED

Higgins marched with clockwork precision, knife-edge creases in his trousers. His posture was rigid, but his heart was mushy as Martha's. For many years, he'd watched with concealed sadness as the Biglum family split apart.

Behind Higgins, three dinner-jacketed members of his serving staff marched with silver domed trays. Sir Biglum sat in his usual place, at the head of the long dining room table. He snapped his fingers and the servers turned in unison, bowed low, and presented his lunch. From roasted hummingbird served with ten savoury sauces to a rack of glazed gazelle, they set dish after dish before him.

Sir Biglum drew the plates closer, hunching over his food. Crumbs exploded from his mouth as his lunch disappeared in sloppy bites. The lunch lasted ten slobbery minutes. After the servers cleared everything away, Higgins enquired, 'May I be of more assistance, sir?'

'In fact, Higgins, you may. Dash off and get Miss Primly. I would like a FULL update on preparations for the bi-quadrennial ball.' Sir Biglum fluttered his fingers at Higgins's retreating back.

*   *   *

Billy and Millicent stood outside the secrets closet. The quarrel inside was still raging.

Billy looked sadly at the door. 'It's my fault.'

'Oh, come on, Billy, it's just the way parents get sometimes. Mine used to have some real storms, but they always ended in a hug. You can't take it too seriously.'

'No, this really *is* my fault. I could have stopped it. They're fighting about Uncle Grim. He tried to yank my soul and send it to the other side.' Billy sighed and waited for Millicent to laugh or scold him.

Instead, she said, 'Billy, you're becoming quite the secrets keeper.' Her eyes brightened in the lantern light. 'And quite the sleuth too. How did you find out?'

Billy told her about the vision and the threat of Nevermore, then leaned his back against the door and slid down to the floor, pulling his knees to his chest. 'What if Uncle Grim tries it again?'

'Will he dare?' Millicent asked. 'Remember, Gossip was there.'

'If it gets around, he'll be in trouble. Judging from the explosion, it was a dark secret.'

'Sounds like it's just what he deserves,' Millicent

said boldly, 'trying to take my best new friend away from me!'

Billy shivered. 'The problem is they'd all get into trouble . . . my parents too. So I'm not sure he'll let it go. And he could show up in any place, at any time.' He frowned at the secrets closet. 'It's all a little confusing for me . . . finding out my parents aren't my real parents, my living mother is old enough to be my grandmother . . . my twin brother is old enough to be my uncle, and I even have a niece that's older than me. On top of it all, now that I'm alive, my skeleton uncle is trying to kill me.'

Millicent stared at Billy. 'You're lucky enough to have two mothers and a father who really love you. Some of us don't have parents around at all!' She folded her arms, turned her back, and buried her cheek in her shoulder. 'I don't think mine will ever come back again.'

Billy slowly got up. He touched her arm and said, 'I'm sorry, Millicent. We can figure out what's tangling up your parents too,' he suggested hopefully.

Millicent smiled and took his hand, 'Maybe we can.'

As the quarrelling voices quietened inside the secrets closet, Billy and Millicent heard new voices, this time through the dining-room wall. They retraced Millicent's steps back through the secret passageway to the spy holes.

'Something's going on in there, Billy. Let's have a peek,' Millicent whispered. They set aside all thoughts of lost parents and murderous uncles and climbed the ladder.

Millicent grabbed the top rung. After a few

minutes Billy pestered her for a turn. 'Come on, Millicent,' he hissed. 'Give someone else a chance.'

'Just a minute,' she whispered back.

Billy fretted as he hung from the ladder. Then he had a clever thought. 'Shove over a bit, I'm going to use this.'

She moved over and peeked out of one eyehole while he reached up with the magic eye to look out of the other.

Higgins and Miss Primly stood before Sir Biglum. They nodded as Sir Biglum listed his latest demands for the ball. 'The crème de la crème will be here, so EVERYTHING must be top-notch. Especially for Lord Pinchly Pennyworth and his daughter, Penelope. Lord Pinchly is the WEALTHIEST man in the realm.'

Miss Primly and Higgins reassured Sir Biglum. He sat back in his chair and closed his eyes. He could see it: the glistening chandeliers and the glittering social elite. He imagined pulling a velvet curtain to reveal the most important painting of the decade. Then his eyes popped opened and he leaned towards his servants. 'Nothing will go wrong or I'll refurbish the family dungeon just for you!'

*   *   *

Billy and Millicent both flinched at Sir Biglum's outburst.

'Oh, Billy. He's a real crank!' Millicent whispered.

While Millicent saw a rather crabby gentleman and his staff in an extraordinarily fancy room, Billy's view was far more disturbing. He could see their souls.

A general goodness radiated from Higgins, but there were a few dark clouds circling around the light. This seemed like the struggle of a normal soul, but Sir Biglum and Miss Primly were another matter. Hers was dark as night thunder, sprouting spidery arms. His was even worse.

When Sir Biglum spoke to Miss Primly about his expectations for the ball, a leering face drifted over his head, floating in a green fog. The piggy manifestation licked its slobbering lips.

Billy eased down the ladder and shakily put the magic eye back into the pouch. He leaned against the wall with a loud *thump*.

Sir Biglum glanced suspiciously at the wall. His withering look gave Millicent a start. She clambered down to Billy and whispered that it was time to go. She didn't have to say it twice. Unfortunately, their lamp flame had gone out. Moving as silently as they could, they began the long, dark trip upstairs.

CHAPTER 22

WITNESS TO UN-MURDER

Commissioner Pickerel had earned his reputation as the most gifted snoop in the Investigative Branch many years before. Despite his height, he was surprisingly stealthy and had unusual talent for a ghost. Just as there are living people with a special talent for seeing the dead, so there are those in the Afterlife with a sharp eye for the living.

Commissioner Pickerel held Gossip in his steel-grey gaze, his face cold as a closed door. He tapped the manifestation's shoulder. It spun around.

Pickerel motioned for Gossip to follow him through a nearby wall.

'You mussst be Commissioner Pickerel. I've been expecting you.' Gossip wound around the commissioner and looked into his eyes. 'I must sssay, I'm delighted to make your acquaintance.

Tell me all about yourself.'

An impatient glance was the only answer. The commissioner flicked a mote of dust off his lapel and began. 'I'm interested in hearing about what you witnessed last night.'

'Oh, dear. We're going to be ssserious, are we?' Gossip stroked the side of the commissioner's lengthy chin, looking as charming as its snaky shape would allow.

'Well, I was making my roundsss, minding my own businessss . . . I had heard that some rather ssssaucy things were going on out in the ssstable . . . when I sssaw the young girl and the ssskeleton boy out for a walk. The next thing I knew, there was sssome kind of explosion. I was a good distance away, so I ssswooped closer. Light was flashing all over the ssskeleton and then a real, live boy was ssstanding there. And not just any boy, mind you, but the one who went missing from the manor yearsss earlier. I'm sure these ssskeletons were responsible.'

'What makes you so sure?'

'The explosion was probably from a sssecret, and then I heard the clattering of ssskeleton bones running.'

'How do closet skeletons turn a skeleton into a boy?'

'Sssimple, dearie. I hear tell that the house has hidden treasure filled with magic. They sssay it's how that sssscoundrel Glass-Eyed Pete made his fortune in the first place. I think those two sssecret keepers got their hands on the magic and turned the young ssskeleton into a living boy. I'll bet it's because they're trying to cover up their earlier crime . . . when they kidnapped his sssoul. It's well

158

passst time we all knew what was going on in that closet.'

Commissioner Pickerel snapped his notebook shut. 'Perhaps we shall, soon enough.'

*   *   *

Millicent had experienced quite enough darkness. She and Billy had been bumping their way up to the attic for what seemed like hours. And they had skinned knees and elbows to prove it.

Billy stopped at a faint light leaking across the floor. He guessed that they were on the third floor. With luck, they could make their way out of the unbearable darkness to the back stairs. Millicent found the latch on the door.

As their eyes adjusted to the light, they discovered Sir Biglum's palatial living room. Billy carefully closed the hidden door. But he wasn't careful enough. Being children and careless of the messy things they leave behind, they didn't see the dusty footprints they tracked on to the room's richly woven carpet.

Billy was impressed with the size of the room, but most interested in the enormous portrait of Sir Biglum. After all, they had started out as identical twins.

The children were looking around the room when they heard voices from the bedroom. They froze.

'I'm sure I could smell it again!' Sir Biglum's voice boomed.

It was followed by another, more hollow in tone, as if it had been mixed with wind and fog. 'My nose has never failed me before. There is something of

159

great value, and it's lurking around here somewhere.'

Millicent went as pale as Mrs Bones. She whispered into Billy's ear, 'I do hope they're not talking about my father's paintings!'

'Could be. I'm going to get a closer look,' Billy said as he fished the magic eye out of its pouch. He peeked the eyeball around the base of the door.

Sir Biglum sat at a desk on the other side of his emperor-sized bed. He was surrounded, as usual, by his factory plans. But something else was there as well.

Greed's green figure floated in front of Sir Biglum, shaking its forefinger. 'If there's money about, we must find it! I have standards, you know. I've been trying to pound that into your head ever since we came to our understanding so many years ago.'

'Quite,' Sir Biglum replied with an uncharacteristic mope.

'You were nothing until I came along. Without me, you'd still be a namby-pamby like your brother . . . too honest and honourable to bear, really! You never would've found the sleeping potion without me, and who would have helped you to lug the sleeping load to the closet?'

'SILENCE!' roared Sir Biglum. 'That's not a time we talk about!'

Billy and Millicent gasped as their wide eyes met.

Sir Biglum rummaged through his papers. 'I'm expecting an update from Hack, Whack and Plunder. Hopefully it's good news. The sale of my brother-in-law's painting will at least pay for the ball. And that should help me snag a few wealthy investors . . . maybe even a wealthy BRIDE. Now be gone. I don't want people thinking I'm as loony as my mother!'

Billy turned to Millicent. He placed a finger over his mouth and pointed to the hallway. They slipped silently away.

*   *   *

A bodyless head floated in front of Dame Biglum and nodded a brisk greeting. 'Afternoon, Madam. My name is Commissioner Pickerel from the Investigative Branch of the Righteousness Department. It's my duty to ask you a few questions.'

'Commissioner Pickerel,' she answered him coldly, 'I'm not a lawyer, but even I suspect that I don't fall under your jurisdiction.'

'True enough, Madam.' The rest of his thin body re-formed as he drifted to her chest of drawers and picked up a portrait of the twins. 'Not at the present time, that is.' While he spoke, he rearranged the objects on its surface. 'I'll guess I'm not the first ghost you've run across in your lifetime?'

'True enough,' she responded, tapping her cane in aggravation.

'In fact, I'll guess ghosts are a regular occurrence for you.'

'Whether they are or not is none of your concern. I wish you to go. I'm an old woman who is, right now, very tired.'

Pickerel glided to a nearby chair. 'I understand how an investigation can be quite inconvenient, Madam, indeed I do . . . all these troublesome

161

questions to answer. But you see, the law's been broken. And the day criminals hold sway over this world and the next . . . you'll find yourself far more inconvenienced. But that aside, I am here to investigate the un-murder of Billy Bones. Do you know the young skeleton, now living boy, in question?'

'Yes, in fact, I do.'

'And how did it happen that you two met?'

Dame Biglum spent the next twenty minutes patiently answering the commissioner's questions truthfully enough, but because of a nibbling mistrust, decided to provide only the most basic of answers. She avoided mentioning her good friend Pete—who she knew had a rascal's reputation in the Afterlife. She also didn't mention that Billy and Millicent had visited her just moments before. In fact, Dame Biglum didn't mention Millicent at all.

Pickerel took notes in a small translucent notebook. As he finished each page it shimmered away, replaced by another. Somewhere in the Afterlife, a filing cabinet grew fuller. When he asked Dame Biglum about her children, Pickerel made a special note to interview Julia Hues. She was, most decidedly, under his jurisdiction.

'Just one more question, then.' The commissioner left his notebook floating in the air as he shook his jammed fountain pen to restart its flow. 'Do you know where I might find young Master Bones?'

'You're not going to take him into custody, are you?'

'That would be quite impossible, given his present state, don't you think?'

'Last I knew, commissioner, my son was visiting his adoptive parents.'

'Adoptive parents,' the ghost snorted. 'Yes, quite.'

Pickerel flipped his notebook closed. But before he departed, Dame Biglum hastily pressed a question of her own. 'Why are you so concerned with an un-murder, as you call it? Wouldn't that be a very good thing?'

'From your perspective, it would look like a very good thing indeed. But from the Investigative Branch's perspective, it means that we have lost control. It is most unnatural, against all laws of the Afterlife and nature. On top of that, it's an unauthorized use of eternal energy. Whoever un-murdered the boy broke at least seven hundred and fifty-five different procedures and regulations.' Commissioner Pickerel's steel-grey eyes hardened more at the thought. He produced a ghostly card that solidified as he handed it to Dame Biglum. 'If you need to contact me,' he said, 'or you remember more details, just burn the card and it will return to me in the Afterlife. I will respond at once. Goodbye . . . for now.'

He pocketed his notebook, capped his pen, and slipped away.

*   *   *

Glass-Eyed Pete bobbed over to Dame Biglum. 'I know how ye be feeling. 'That Pickerel gives me goosebumps as well.'

Pickerel may have been a stealthy ghost, but the old pirate had a few tricks of his own. He had been spying on the interrogation from inside a picture frame.

Dame Biglum looked up. 'Oh, Peter, I'm so worried for Billy. Do you think we can help?'

'Most of those investigator dunderheads don't know a poop deck from a paddle. But this feller looked sharper than most.'

'With any luck he'll be as bumbling as the rest.'

'Aye, I hope so too. But I'll stand watch on that fellow. Maybe I should raise a warning to the Boneses.' He patted her shoulder. 'Hold fast there, Maddy, I'll see what I can do.'

Dame Biglum raised a weary hand to the disappearing pirate and sat heavily back in her chair.

*   *   *

Billy and Millicent tiptoed farther down the hallway and took refuge in a nearby bedroom. 'It makes me wonder what I could be capable of, Millicent. He is my identical twin.'

'Not *that* identical,' Millicent replied, stroking her forehead. She'd been lost in thought since they entered the room. 'We need to get up to the attic to warn Grandmother Maddy . . .'

Billy agreed wholeheartedly. He turned to go, but Millicent was still caught up in thought. 'Uncle Barkley locked you in the closet and left you to die,' she said. 'But why? He's the heir to the Biglum fortune. He was going to get everything anyway. It doesn't make sense.'

'I must say, Millicent, my brother and Miss Primly have the most disgusting-looking souls.'

Millicent looked up in surprise. 'You saw their souls? Another secret you're keeping from me,

Billy Bones! You could take over the closet any day now.'

'Right, except I just spilled the beans again.'

'Well, you can't expect to become an expert overnight. Let's get back up to the attic. Should we take the secret way?'

Neither explorer had much appetite for facing the dark passage again. They agreed to carry emergency candles and matches on their next outing. They crept silently back through the hallway toward the servants' stairwell.

Millicent stopped to make sure no one was nearby as Billy continued on. She was trailing Billy up to the fourth floor when she heard Miss Primly's barbed-wire voice. 'Where have you been off to? You think you can wander around my house on a whim? You putrid little carbuncle!'

With that, Miss Primly exploded after Millicent. Oh, but she was fast as a spider with a moth caught in its web! Millicent banged up the stairs as fast as she could. Billy heard the commotion down below and sped to Millicent's room. He frantically looked for something to use against Miss Primly. The cracked pitcher was the first thing he saw.

He grabbed it, rushed back to the stairwell, and readied his aim. Millicent rounded the fourth-floor banister and streaked towards the next set of stairs. She bit her lip in effort as her legs pumped up the remaining steps. Miss Primly thundered around the corner like eight-legged lightning.

Billy let go. A white blur whipped over Millicent's head and crashed into the raging housekeeper's forehead. The pitcher exploded into a cloud of shards. Billy shouted, 'Hurry, Millicent!'

Miss Primly wobbled for an instant. Her eyes narrowed when she saw Billy. 'You!' she yelled. Primly pounced, but before she could grab them, both children floated into the air. They swung by the scruff of their necks as they were swooped away like stolen goods.

Whether Miss Primly or the children were more surprised is hard to say. They flew up the stairs and around the post. Primly flashed up the stairs in pursuit.

Back in the attic, doors crashed open before the children as they whooshed feet first down the next hallway, past the rocking horse and into Dame Biglum's bedroom. The door slammed behind them just as Miss Primly sprinted into the playroom.

Dame Biglum's eyes popped open at all the slamming and crashing. She hadn't expected Pete to return so quickly.

Pete put Billy and Millicent down and threw his shoulder to the door. He gasped, 'Looks like it were a lucky stroke me and Jenkins happened by.'

'I should say!' Billy agreed. The children piled everything they could move against the door.

Primly whirled up, the folds of her black dress swirling. She pushed the door; the more pressure she applied, the more was returned.

Rubbing the growing welt on her forehead, she banged her fist on the door, and shouted, 'I don't know how you did it, all this flying about. But I know one thing for certain: you won't do it any more. At least nowhere else in *this* manor!'

She thrust a key into Dame Biglum's door and twisted it like she was wringing a neck.

Commissioner Pickerel's fingers were long and thin like white wax candles. He used one now to tap his chin as he perched uncomfortably on a small chest and contemplated Mr and Mrs Bones.

Arms crossed defiantly, Mr Bones stared back. Mrs Bones paced nervously, throwing razor-sharp glares towards the commissioner. One could almost hear the friction crackling in the air.

Commissioner Pickerel began again. 'As I mentioned before, the Investigative Branch needs more background on this most unusual case, and this so-called adopted son of yours.' The commissioner's usually impenetrable features were clearly angry.

Mr Bones answered. 'You know that's out of the question. If you want any documents, you'll need a warrant from the Moral Authority.'

'Then you leave me no choice but to throw this matter up to the Authority. They'll be happy to drag your chief skeleton, Oversecretary Underhill, into court.'

'Go ahead. Handing over secret documents is against procedure. Even the oversecretary can't do anything about that.'

'We'll see.' The commissioner crossed his long arms. 'It is quite clear, however, that you are both at fault in this situation.'

Mr Bones leaned forward. 'How do you figure that?'

'You let the boy out of the secrets closet, didn't you?'

'There's no crime in that. He's not a member of the department.'

167

'According to the Travel Charters, "Any spirit, ghost, skeleton or otherwise deceased person shall not disturb the peace and tranquillity of the living." You let him out. You are responsible for the mayhem he caused.'

'As far as we can make out, Commissioner,' Mr Bones growled, 'the only tranquillity he disturbed belongs to the Investigative Branch. And, I might point out, now that he's alive, you have no case.'

Skeletons are exceptionally good at stony stares. Their hardened features lend themselves so well to it.

But the commissioner was unmoved. 'Bones, the law's been broken, and we know you and your wife were involved. A witness at the scene of the un-murder is pointing a finger at you.'

Lars Bones shot to his feet. 'You, you . . . LIAR!'

'I don't see any documentation to that effect, do you, Mr Bones? Furthermore, seeing how uncooperative you two have been with the Investigative Branch, you'll be lucky if you're not charged with treason as well.'

Mrs Bones stopped pacing—she looked stricken. Her husband yelled, 'We've spent nearly our whole afterlives in government service!'

Commissioner Pickerel snapped his fingers, and several smoky wisps swirled through the floorboards and walls. As the vapours spun slowly in the air, menacing smiles emerged and twisted into thuggish Afterlife officers. 'Now, I think it's time you two come with me. We have some lovely accommodation waiting for you until we see fit to handle your case.'

168

'You can't—' Mr Bones sputtered.

'Oh dear, my good man, I seem to be overstepping my authority,' Pickerel smirked. He caught the eye of a sergeant and nodded towards Mr Bones. 'Tie him up first.'

In the back of the closet, Mrs Bones dipped her quill into an inkwell and scratched her signature on to the official departmental memo she had been quietly penning. She calmly folded the memo and slipped it among the other papers on her small writing desk. Then she jumped up, rounding the desk in a fury. 'When Lord Underhill hears of this, you'll be the one in shackles!'

'He certainly won't be hearing it from you,' snarled Commissioner Pickerel.

'He'll hear, Commissioner, and *you'll* be sorry he did.'

'You tell him, Decette! If Pickerel and his flunkies think they can intimidate us, they're sorely mistaken.' Commissioner Pickerel's squad tied Mr Bones's arms behind his back.

They clamped Mr and Mrs Bones into leg irons and marched them through a glowing portal. As the closet resettled into darkness, the door groaned open—leaving the closet exposed to any wandering eye.

CHAPTER 23

ATTIC PRISONERS

Millicent had spent hours staring out of the window. It was clear the Biglum ball was fast approaching. Grocer, cheese merchant and wine shop wagons had been streaming to the manor all afternoon.

At that moment, three horse-drawn wagons with *Smuggly and Sons. Fine Gourmet Cuisine. Pleasing refined palates since 1833* painted on their sides were clomping up to the manor. An older man snapped the reins of the first wagon. His stomach proudly advertised his high opinion of his wares. Millicent guessed he must be Mr Smuggly. The drivers of the second and third wagons were younger copies of the first. *The 'and Sons', of course*. She watched them disappear around the side of the manor.

'Millicent, could you light the candles, m'dear?' Dame Biglum's voice was low, for fear of waking

Billy. He was asleep in her bed, making up for his miserable night before. Pete was asleep too. The effort of carrying the children had left him faint, but he refused to leave them. He floated in a wingback chair, his body bobbing with ghostly snores.

Millicent always enjoyed lighting and putting out candles. She was fascinated to see flames unwind from a match head. And she also liked to see the flames whooshed off to sleep when she blew them out, leaving their smoky trails drifting up to the Afterlife.

She blinked back a tear at the thought of her parents. She wished the smoke were a string she could use to pull them back to this world. She missed them so much.

Dame Biglum guessed where Millicent's thoughts were leading her and tried her own hand at reeling the girl back. 'Come sit by me.' She thumped the cushion next to her. 'What's wrong, my dear?'

Millicent told her everything, from her parents' first visits back in the loft to their most recent visit only a few days before. She told her of Gossip's cruel remarks. And she finished by asking, 'Do they really not care? Are they too busy for me?'

Dame Biglum closed her eyes for a long minute and then said, 'Millicent, the fact that they came in the first place means their love for you is stronger than thc wall between the two worlds. Something must be holding them up.

'As to the horrid things Gossip said, Julia left here with my blessing. More than that, really. I asked her to leave. I didn't want to see another life wasted in this manor.'

'So nothing Gossip said was true?' Relief fizzed through Millicent like root beer.

'Gossip wouldn't know truth if it tap-danced on Gossip's head!' Dame Biglum stroked Millicent's wild curls. 'I only wish I could have seen Julia too. But that's just a selfish old woman talking.' She sighed and continued, 'I've never found time to thank you, my dear. And more's the shame on me, as my life is not exactly bustling with activity, stuck away up here in the attic.'

'Thank me for what?'

'It's a great thing that you've given me, dear. More precious than any buried treasure . . . you've given me *hope*.' She caressed Millicent's cheek. 'Your being here is a magnificent gift in many ways. I'm sure your parents feel that way as well.'

Millicent squeezed even closer. 'I miss them.'

'Oh, my dear, I miss them too!'

Dame Biglum's wrinkled hand enveloped Millicent's and held it quietly for a long time.

That's how Scamp found them as he scuttled under the door and into the room.

*   *   *

Sir Biglum sat in his study, grinding his teeth on a cigar. Twiddling a calling card in his chubby fingers, he shifted the cigar in his mouth and examined his plans.

A crisp knock roused his attention. Higgins entered the room carrying a refilled wine glass and more cigars. Sir Biglum grunted towards a side table.

Higgins carefully set down his load and was about to ease out of the room when Sir Biglum

172

finally spoke. 'HIGGINS, I want to see Miss Primly down here right away. A blazing baboon's bottom could do a better job than she's been doing!'

Higgins nodded. He bolted down the hallway like a sprung clock spring.

*   *   *

Billy yawned and stretched his arms one after the other like he was delivering slow-motion punches. His fleshy arms felt heavy, but the stretch unkinked several spots with a pop. Billy opened his eyes to a vision of candlelight shining through a ghostly body. Pete stood smiling only a few metres away.

'We were wondering when ye was going to surface again.' Pete winked as he tossed off the bed quilt. 'Now, hit the deck. Maddy's got something to say.'

Billy bounded out of bed, and Pete led him to the couch. As they passed, the candle flames bent forward and seemed eager to listen too. Scamp jumped into Billy's hand with excited chirps. Pete seated his great-many-greats grandson next to Millicent, then leaned on the couch back while Dame Biglum addressed the room.

'Now, my dears, I'm thinking it's time I did something useful. I've spent far too much time hiding away up here.' Dame Biglum swung her cane like a sword. 'Pete, why don't you pass through the door and unlock it. Then we can get down to business.'

'Sounds like a fine plan, Maddy, but there be a few rough spots. I can get through the door, like ye

173

say, but even a ghost needs a key to unlock a door . . .' Pete shoved his hands in his pockets and drifted to the window, lost for a moment in thought. 'Maybe I can steal the key from Primly's pocket. Best we wait a touch before we all march down. The day after tomorrow should do it, I think.' He drew the curtain aside and watched a grocer's cart clatter away from the manor.

Millicent joined him at the window. Even in the darkness, she could read *Smuggly and Sons*. The thought of a delicious banquet with stacks of food leaped into her mind. They hadn't had a thing to eat or drink since morning. Then, just as suddenly, she knew what Pete was thinking. 'The Biglum ball!'

'Now that's a plan!' Dame Biglum thumped her cane. 'I'll march in and confront my son when he's least expecting it and has the most to lose. Oh, this will take him down quite a few notches.'

'I'll shove off right now for the key,' Pete said. 'Be back before ye can say Biglum's yer uncle.' He winked at Millicent and melted through the floor.

Billy's heart quickened. He knew he had to be brave.

*   *   *

Higgins delivered a panting Miss Primly and then bowed out of the study again. Miss Primly approached Sir Biglum's desk like she was facing final judgement. Sir Biglum was well aware she was there, but was content to let her sweat it out while he shifted through his papers. She stood in silence.

Sir Biglum savoured his cigar for a few more puffs, laid it in the ashtray, and finally looked up.

174

He put his elbows on the desk and rested his chin on interwoven fingers. 'Well, Miss Primly, about that ruckus in the attic, what do you have to say for yourself?' he asked quietly.

Miss Primly blinked, surprised by his calmness. 'Well, sir, I'm—'

'SHUT YOUR GOB SPOUT!' Sir Biglum exploded. 'A TOENAIL CLIPPING could keep better control of this house! That racket was inexcusable. I'll have you know, you're not just sacked, you're triple-sacked. Your whole career's taken a TWIRL DOWN THE BOG! You will most certainly NEVER WORK AGAIN as a housekeeper, and when I'm finished with you, you won't even be able to get a job as a BEGGAR IN BOMBAY!'

Miss Primly stood stunned as Sir Biglum paused for a secret smile. He was enjoying himself and really didn't intend to fire Miss Primly, at least not until after the ball.

'You're a disgrace to Miss Foxly's School for Extraordinary Housekeepers . . .'

Just over Miss Primly's shoulder, Sir Biglum caught the sight of a familiar translucent face as it peered through a Biglum family portrait, then quickly retreated. He would have missed it, had it not been for a ghostly parrot squawk.

Miss Primly finally worked up enough courage to respond. 'It was your niece, sir . . .'

'Blaming the whole thing on someone else, eh? That's HIGHLY vicious! But quaintly corrupt.' Sir Biglum smiled. 'Tell me more.'

'. . . And there was a stranger. A little boy I'd never seen before.'

'A little boy?'

175

'Yes, sir, a chubby little boy. I locked him up in Dame Biglum's room too.'

'Locked him up, hmmm . . . Have the key, do you?' Sir Biglum held out his hand, fingers wiggling expectantly.

Miss Primly nervously rummaged in her pocket then paled. 'It's . . . it's gone!'

Instead of loosing a fiery reprisal for lost keys and letting strangers into the household, Sir Biglum calmly asked Miss Primly to fetch his twelve-gauge boxlock shotgun. She was very happy to help.

Walking towards the portrait, Sir Biglum casually drew on a pair of felt gloves. 'Well now, PETE, it's been a long time,' he clucked as he fingered the parchment calling card in his palm.

Pete emerged from the wall. 'Ye scurvy rat, I trusted ye with all me secrets and ye stabs me in the back by slamming us into that trunk!'

Jenkins stared dirks and daggers from his unpatched eye.

'It's too bad we don't have time to discuss it in all its intriguing details. But someone is DEAD set on meeting you.' A lopsided smile leaped to Sir Biglum face. He held up the calling card, puffed his cigar to fire up the ash, and held the glowing tip to an edge. The card flamed and burst into nothingness. An instant later, the air around Sir Biglum glowed and stirred. Out stepped Commissioner Pickerel.

He lurched forward, but Pete dodged and snuffed out of reality. Pickerel grunted and followed. The air sparkled with their exits just as Miss Primly trotted into the room with the shotgun.

'RIGHT. I'll take that.' Sir Biglum grabbed the gun, cracked it open, and pretended to examine it. 'Thanks ever so much. It struck me that this thing needs a good cleaning—especially since you've smeared it with your greasy fingers.' A sly smile skinned his face. 'Now why don't you get back to making sure that the ball comes off without a hitch. If it doesn't . . . consider our previous discussion just a WARM-UP!'

Miss Primly left the room balancing confusion with relief as Sir Biglum gathered up an assortment of shotgun shells and stuffed them in his pocket.

CHAPTER 24

THE MARCH INTO DARKNESS

Billy, Millicent and Dame Biglum jumped as two ragged holes exploded through the old woman's door, one where the lock had been and the other right next to it. The door creaked open.

Sir Biglum sauntered in, calmly reloading his gun. 'I DO hate it when I mislay my keys. Oh well, nothing a bit of armament can't fix. Don't look so SHOCKED, Mother. I'm sure you'd say yourself that a son should visit every decade or so.' He turned to Billy and blinked his eyes in feigned shock. 'Say, look who's here. Your long-lost son. ISN'T this a surprise?'

Dame Biglum hugged Billy tightly and thrust a defiant chin towards Sir Biglum.

Sir Biglum chuckled and pulled back the twin hammers of the boxlock with a double *thunk*. 'We're all going on a bit of a march. And let's not think about escape, children.'

As they turned to go, Sir Biglum noticed a scrap of paper peeking out of Millicent's sleeve.

'Let's have it.' Sir Biglum waved his gun in Millicent's pale face. 'That paper.'

He swiped it out of her hand and then, with shotgun tucked into the crook of his arm, patted down Millicent and Billy, searching for anything else of interest. He found nothing more on Millicent but was thrilled to find Billy's pouch with the magic eye and medallion.

*   *   *

Tucked away in Millicent's wavy hair, Scamp had observed everything. He watched Sir Biglum lead the grim procession down the secret staircase and through the secret hallways, toward the secrets closet.

'Looks like I'll have to tell EVERYONE that you're extending your travels indefinitely, Mother. Of course I WON'T tell them that you'll be exploring the hills and dales of the Afterlife.'

Dame Biglum straightened her back and walked stiffly ahead. 'You have been a great disappointment to me, Barkley.'

Sir Biglum grunted out a laugh, 'That's RICH coming from a mother who can't even tell her children apart. Very rich, indeed.'

'You were so very much alike.'

'Well, as you can tell by now, we COULDN'T have been more different. But I did have quite a talent for fooling you.' Sir Biglum turned to Billy and continued. 'Imagine my surprise, dear Brother, when Commissioner Pickerel mentioned to me that you were out and about. Oh, YES,' he turned back to his mother, 'he questioned me as well.' Then he motioned to his brother. 'I had my suspicions that something was afoot behind these secret walls again, and I suspected it was my little niece here, but I couldn't figure for the LIFE of me who owned the other set of footprints. You really ought not to drag dust around like that . . . so messy.'

Millicent glanced at Billy while Sir Biglum continued. 'Of course I knew Glass-Eyed Pete had a hand in this. I discovered the opened chest DAYS ago. But soon you'll all be on the other side and I'll have the ENTIRE Biglum estate to myself.' He grunted another murky laugh. 'Ah, here we are at your FINAL destination.'

Sir Biglum seemed puzzled that the closet door was already opened. He motioned the children and his mother inside. Billy and Millicent clutched Dame Biglum's black skirts as they huddled into the closet behind her.

A few secrets stirred sullenly as they entered. But to Billy's horror, there was no trace of Mr and Mrs Bones.

Dame Biglum glared at her son. 'If you think Pete could be a thorn in your side, wait until I'm gone. You'll see how I'm going to haunt you.'

'Yes, but NOT likely with the special arrangements that I have with Commissioner Pickerel. And if you think Glass-Eyed Pete is going to get you out of this pickle, think again. I'm sure the good Commissioner Pickerel has him SECURELY in Nevermore by now.' Sir Biglum held the back of his hand up to his forehead in a mockery of sadness.

Billy flushed with anger and took a step forward,

but quickly retreated when Sir Biglum swung the boxlock in his direction.

Ever since Sir Biglum entered the closet, he had been sniffing like a bloodhound. He held up his lamp and nosed one of the trunks with the tip of his shotgun. He flipped the top opened to reveal Artemis Hues's wondrous paintings. Seaside colours splashed over wall slats and beams. The painting on top was the one that had captivated Billy so completely. Even Sir Biglum seemed briefly charmed.

'Those are mine!' shrieked Millicent.

'Not any more.' Her uncle smirked. 'I have the claims slip. I say! Look at all these . . . each one worth a FORTUNE. I have a whole new opinion of your father. I used to think he was a lowly, miserable SCAB. Now I think of him as a lowly, miserable scab who could PAINT.' He savoured the paintings as he uncovered them. 'These will all do nicely.'

As Sir Biglum dragged the trunks out of the closet, Billy whispered to Millicent, 'Don't worry, I'll bet anything Pete can get away.' But he wasn't so sure.

Several more trunks rattled as their secrets stirred to life. Sir Biglum was linked to most of these lies and secrets in one way or another. They woke as if their father had just entered the room.

Sir Biglum turned for one last time to gloat.

Dame Biglum snapped, 'The estate was always yours, Barkley. You were firstborn, even if it was by a minute. Your brother—' she paused and looked at Billy—'was going to have to live by your good graces all along. Why are you doing this?'

Biglum glared at her. 'Mother, you still don't

recognize me after all these years. SUCH a shame. *I'M* Goodwin. *HE*—' the false Sir Biglum jabbed a thumb towards Billy—'is Barkley. The ENTIRE fortune was going to go to Mr Namby-Pamby here, not to the more deserving twin, namely MYSELF. And how fast would our fortune have been frittered away by HIS caring heart? The local charities would have been flush with cash his first week!'

At that moment, Billy's heart was filled with much more than caring. Rage was beating in thunderous bumps. He wanted nothing more than to fling himself at his awful twin. But Millicent held him by the flap of his sailor suit.

Dame Biglum stared in horror. 'Goodwin?' she croaked.

'Now it's too late.' Goodwin stepped back into the corridor and pulled at the glowing skeleton key still in the lock. It didn't budge. He redoubled his efforts.

Billy took Millicent's hand and whispered, 'He's told so many lies, looks like he's forgotten how to tell the truth.'

Millicent smiled at Billy and they both prayed he wouldn't remember. Veins popped out in Goodwin's neck as he strained. The key shuddered but wouldn't let go of its hook. Then, to Billy and Millicent's disappointment, the panting Goodwin finally told a truth.

'I hope these three kick the bucket quietly, but not quickly.' He caught the key out of the air and stuffed it in his pocket. Breathing heavily, he leaned on his shotgun.

Billy stepped forward. 'You won't get away with this.'

Millicent tried to shush him, but Sir Biglum only laughed. 'Won't I though? If anyone decides to investigate, they'll only find a trail leading to Miss Primly. She was good enough to cover this shotgun with fingerprints.'

Every secret in the closet was wide awake now. Trunk locks rattled as they strained to get out, but the black-hearted Goodwin W. Biglum was too quick. He slammed the door with an echoing boom. The door's lock squeaked. Stacks of trunks lurched forward and tipped, pounding the door as they fell.

When the trunks settled down, Billy, Millicent, Scamp and Dame Biglum were left in a deep, thick darkness filled with thinning hopes.

CHAPTER 25

THE BALL

When Miss Primly sent out invitations to the grand Biglum ball, nearly all the guests replied 'yes'. The late August date meant the event would be the final curtain call of the summer social calendar, and there was a buzz of expectation. Society's fanciest and most powerful planned to close the season with a bang.

They had no idea how exactly their wishes would be granted.

The manor was a hornet's nest of activity. Miss Primly and Higgins were well beyond exhaustion. They shouted orders, directed deliveries, and did not take even a moment to rest, especially not now. For tonight every candle, gas jet and chandelier would be lit, every decorative dollop and morsel of food would be prepared by the greatest chefs in the country, and the ballroom would be readied for one hundred of the highest ranking guests, not to mention eighty members of the Royal Philharmonic.

Already the best bedrooms had been aired, dusted, and stacked with luggage of the bluest bluebloods. There were satchels from His Excellency, carpetbags from the prime minister, and steamer trunks from the wealthiest man in the realm, Lord Pinchly Pennyworth. He shared a suite with his horse-faced daughter, Penelope. She was his only child.

Sir Biglum (really Goodwin, but the rest of the world still knew him as Sir Biglum) checked and rechecked with Miss Primly and Higgins on the special care they were taking with the Pennyworths. So much depended on Miss Penelope and her gilded fortune.

With all of the chaos, no one paid much attention to Sir Biglum's apologies that his mother and Millicent were away on vacation.

*   *   *

Scamp did notice Sir Biglum's lies as they popped into existence all over and fluttered down around his head. With nobody to sort and file, they began to stack up. Scamp was the only one comfortable in the darkness. His bug vision worked quite well, but the sight of his fellow cellmates saddened him. They sat on the floor, draped against stacked chests. Scamp tried rolling a dust ball into Billy's hand, but he pulled it away and sighed. The boy rubbed his empty belly, pressed his head between his knees and gently sobbed. He wasn't used to all the aches and pains of a living body, especially hunger.

Not being very wise in the ways of humans, Scamp had never seen someone cry. At first he though Billy was laughing (an easy mistake with shoulders shaking and muffled sounds). But when a juicy tear splashed on his head, Scamp retreated a few steps.

Billy, Millicent and Dame Biglum had long ago stopped talking. Their only sounds were muffled sobs and sighs.

Their sadness felt so real, so cold—almost like it was staring him in the face. And the next thing Scamp knew, it was!

Something dark enough to strain his bug vision rose up through the floorboards. Cold, heartless, with two glossy eyes floating in an empty hood, it drifted towards the boy. Scamp's antennae twittered with alarm. Billy fell limp as it approached like his body was being sucked dry.

Scamp didn't know how long his friend could last against this creature. But what could he do? The tiny beetle scuttled in a circle, searching in desperation. Mr and Mrs Bones were gone and it would be a long time before Mr Benders would be back. Scamp chittered nervously to himself, drawing the attention of the shadowy creature. It considered him for a moment, then continued drifting towards Billy.

'Ah ha!' Scamp shouted in Bug. There was someone else who visited the closet—another family member, Billy's Uncle Grim. But Scamp's excitement didn't last long. There is only one sure way for the living to call Grim, and it involved the biggest sacrifice of all.

Scamp's antennae wilted as he bowed his head. A moment later he squared all four shoulders, smiled at Billy for the last time, and turned to face Despair.

*   *   *

In the grand dining room, empty stomachs were the last thing on anybody's mind as the guests pushed their chairs back. The ten-course meal had been a marvel (and they had the bulging paunches to prove it).

It was time to move on to the drawing rooms. The women withdrew in sashays of silk and bustles, and the men in clouds of cigar smoke. There was much to discuss in the realms of wealth, politics, sport and fashion. So everyone divided into chummy cliques.

As host, Sir Biglum's duty was to circulate, but he was interested only in Lord Pennyworth. Unfortunately, Lord Pennyworth's only reason for attending was to please his daughter, Penelope. He divided his time between acquiring mountains of money and doting on her, which left absolutely no time for the likes of his host.

Sir Biglum could barely contain his drool as he smelt the gobs of cash lining the wealthy financier's pockets. He was talented at smelling fortunes, but Lord Pinchly Pennyworth was even more talented at smelling intruders.

'SO, Lord Pennyworth,' Biglum began, 'tell me of your cattle holdings in Argentina.'

Lord Pennyworth looked him up and down. 'Quite,' he said, and looked away.

Biglum frowned and tried again. 'I hear, Lord Pennyworth, that the copper market is about to be CORNERED.'

Lord Pennyworth responded: 'Indeed,' then turned his back and struck up a conversation with a friend.

Sir Biglum retreated to a side table and replotted his strategy. Greed's withering voice whispered into his ear, 'Imagine, he comes into this house to eat, smoke, and drain your port dry, then he has the brass to turn his back on you!'

Sir Biglum tapped his fist on the humidor holding his finest cigars. He lit one and puffed furious clouds of smoke. The Biglums had been begging for social standing for too long. He studied Lord Pennyworth's back and banged the cigar box flat. Several guests lifted eyebrows and then turned away.

Forget the arrogant old devil, he vowed to himself. *Just wait for the dancing, then sweep the girl off her feet. He may not listen to you, but he has a soft spot for her—even with that horsey face of hers.*

A sly grin unknotted Sir Biglum's frown. He took a few self-satisfied puffs of his cigar. *Penelope Pennyworth, prepare to meet the all-school WALTZ champion of Miss Palindrome's School of Ballroom Dance and Manners.*

*   *   *

Billy shivered. He felt so cold, so lonely, so lost. He slumped against Dame Biglum, but she too was cold as clay. An imagined picture of Nevermore drifted into his thoughts. Billy felt sorry for himself, but more worried for his skeleton parents. What if they were already trapped in the darkness of that horrid place?

How did it get so cold in here? More thoughts

stumbled through his mind. *And how can pitch black look even blacker? Something's here . . . and whatever it is, it's coming closer.*

Billy was beyond caring, until he heard a sharp trill right in front of him.

Scamp chittered, 'Stop right there, shadow! Back your rear end out of this closet before I back it out for you!'

What's he thinking? That thing feels way bigger than a beetle! A cold, bleak laugh echoed through the closet, prompting Scamp to shout more insect threats.

'Scamp, be careful!' Billy cried out hoarsely.

A trunk clattered, then another chittering insult. Millicent and Dame Biglum stirred now.

'Scamp!' Billy wailed, lurching forward on wobbly legs. He picked his way through jumbled trunks. The dark thing hissed angrily and tossed more trunks aside. Billy heard Scamp skitter across the floor, then a whoosh of cold anger, a thud and a crunch.

'Scamp! No!' Billy sobbed, sinking to his knees. He scrabbled around on the floor, desperately searching for the remains of his oldest friend.

*   *   *

Wearing her very best black velvet dress, Miss Primly stood behind two crimson and gold-flocked curtains. This room was easily the most extravagant in all the manor. The stonework circled a first-storey walkway that curved into two staircases down to the dance floor. Marble floor tiles spiralled in graceful curves around the gold Biglum crest in the centre of the room. From her hidden post, she could see every glittering aristocrat as they strutted and preened.

As she adjusted the curtains, she observed Sir Biglum's interest in Miss Penelope Pennyworth. Biglum bowed to Miss Pennyworth, took her in his arms, and weaved her between the other stately couples swirling on the dance floor.

Miss Primly's smile bit into her face. It looked like her boss had found his filly. She pulled the curtains closed and rushed off to check that everything else was running smoothly. And for now it was—smooth as shoe polish.

*   *   *

'What's happened?' Millicent croaked.

Dame Biglum whispered, 'Billy? Are you all right?'

'That cold, dark thing killed Scamp!' Billy shouted. Fresh tears streamed down his cheeks.

'How?' Millicent climbed weakly over the trunks and slumped next to Billy.

'It . . . it crushed him,' Billy sobbed.

Seconds later, the floor vibrated as something enormous pounded into the secret hallway and stopped outside the closet door. There was a murmur and a pawing. Blue light bathed the door, then it groaned open. Black sparks of eternal energy skipped across the room as Fleggs shook his mane and whinnied a greeting.

Before they could draw another breath, Millicent and Dame Biglum froze. Time stopped.

But it kept ticking for Billy as darks sparks crackled out of his body and surrounded him. He was surprised to see his bones glowing beneath his skin. His skeleton vision returned.

Then Billy was gripped by another force.

Terror.

He scuttled backwards, slamming into the writing desk. Papers flew, some landing in his lap.

Grim entered the closet. He took a few steps and glanced at the floor. A blue spark from Scamp's crushed remains drifted slowly into the air. Grim caught the tiny light as it floated by and twirled his finger, making a bug-sized opening to the Afterlife.

'I know someone who will be very sad that it was your time,' Grim spoke solemnly, scooting the glimmering dot through. He closed the hole and, with a clockwise hand gesture, restarted time.

He turned to Billy and offered him a hand.

Billy flinched. 'Leave me alone!' he whispered.

Grim hunkered down to the boy's level. 'You've lost a good friend, and I'm sorry. But I'm not here to take you, Billy. I want to help.'

'Why should he believe you?' Millicent cried. 'You tried to kill him once already!'

Before Grim answered, he produced a glowing ball of white light. He released it, and it floated to the rafters so that his accuser could see him better. He pulled his hood back and turned towards Millicent. His eyes dimmed with wistful sadness. 'Billy had been suffering greatly in this very closet. And I extended his stay on Earth much longer than I had a right to.' He told her how Mr and Mrs Bones had longed for a child and how he had granted their request at considerable danger to them all.

Millicent held her tongue, but also a few suspicions. It hadn't been so long ago he'd tried to take her friend.

Grim turned back to Billy. 'I'm sorry. Your friend is right. I am responsible for much of this mess. Let me help you sort it out.'

Billy nodded cautiously and explained how they'd been guided to the closet by Sir Biglum's shotgun, how the Boneses were gone, and how Scamp had been crushed by Despair.

Grim listened carefully. When Billy finished, Grim stood up and picked his way through the trunks. He scooped something off the floor, then returned and gently tucked Scamp's tiny remains in Billy's hand. 'He could have left this closet at any time to save himself. Instead he chose to stay. Without this good fellow's bravery, I wouldn't be here to save you.'

Billy solemnly folded the remains of his friend in his handkerchief and placed it in his pocket. He knew his friend deserved as noble a funeral as any king, and promised he'd do his best.

As he shifted position, the papers slipped off his lap. Grim was about to place them back on the writing desk when one stopped him.

Grim looked up. 'It's from your mother, Billy.' He glanced at Dame Biglum, then back to Billy. 'Decette . . . They've been arrested and sent back to the Afterlife. She says Commissioner Pickerel and his goons are behind this. She points out, and I agree, that Commissioner Pickerel has grossly overstepped his authority.' Grim refolded the document and stuck it in his hip pocket. This time, it was his smile that lit the closet. 'Seems she was hoping Mr Benders would find it . . . This piece of evidence will go a long way towards putting Pickerel in his place. His favourite place:

Nevermore.'

'I have a bit more proof, if you would like it,' Dame Biglum offered. She pulled a handkerchief out of her sleeve. Tucked inside was Commissioner Pickerel's card. She handed it to Grim timidly, not wanting to touch the hand of Death.

Grim winked. 'It takes more than a quick touch to send you on your way.' He tucked the card alongside the letter and turned towards the door. 'I must get back to the Afterlife straight away.'

This time, Billy didn't flinch when his skeleton uncle put a hand on his shoulder. 'Billy, it's going to be a tricky business in front of the High Council, but I'm going to do everything I can. Will you find a way to forgive me?'

The promise of his skeleton parents' return softened Billy's anger. But he couldn't quite bring himself to say anything.

Grim leaned closer. 'I may have to admit my misdeeds up there. If I don't see you again, just know I'll miss you.' Grim searched Billy's face for the smallest smile. And that's what he got. It was skinny, to be sure, but it was enough. He mounted Fleggs. The horse reared and pounded back to the other side of existence.

Dame Biglum thumped towards the door. 'Sounds like the ball is in full swing. Your brother awaits, Billy.'

'I bet these will really get his attention.' Billy shoved one of the trunks into the hallway.

'Brilliant!' Millicent exclaimed. She jumped up to help him push.

*   *   *

It had taken all their effort to move only three trunks into the dining room. There were many more behind, but Billy, Millicent and Dame Biglum were weak with hunger. They sat on the trunks and tried to gather what little strength they had left. That was where Higgins found them. The butler and his crew were on their way to the foyer with trays of refreshments for the coachmen.

Higgins was shocked to see the sad state of the escapees. 'Dame Biglum! Madam, may we be of service?'

'Indeed you may, Higgins. If you wouldn't mind bringing those trays a bit closer, we could put them to good use.'

'Certainly!' Higgins gestured to his crew and they swarmed forward with their trays. The children and old lady greedily tore into the finger food and punch.

When the trio slowed down, Higgins asked, 'May I ask what happened to you? You look as though you've been sorely used.'

'Just how sorely used you will find out shortly, if you will help us with these trunks. There are a good many more through that sideboard entrance and a short walk down that dark hall.'

'Certainly, Madam. Gentlemen?'

Soon more than forty trunkloads of the manor's secrets were stacked at the back of the ballroom landing.

CHAPTER 26

THE TRUTH HURTS

On this late August evening, it was clear to all: Sir Biglum had been shot in the heart by Cupid's arrow. And the object of his desire was sweeping around the dance floor in his arms. Not the girl— he didn't care one penny for her. It was all those other pennies that he adored. In his mind, he wasn't dancing with the plainest girl in the kingdom; he was dancing with a bank vault, the plumpest and prettiest one imaginable.

Just before midnight, he whispered something in her ear. Penelope Pennyworth cried out, cross-eyed with excitement. Sir Biglum shooed the conductor off the stage and took his place. The orchestra quickly ended the song.

He held up his hands and addressed the room. 'Lords, ladies and honoured guests, I have an ANNOUNCEMENT to make!'

'As do I!'

All eyes turned. Dame Biglum, tired and dusty but with her head held high, was descending the curved staircase.

'I present to you: Dame Biglum of Houndstooth-on-Codswattle,' Higgins announced proudly from the top of the stairs. There was no orchestra to accompany this introduction, only a patter of curious applause from the crowd—and Sir Biglum's stunned expression.

'Now, Goodwin. And it is Goodwin, by the way, not Sir Biglum, as you all might have imagined. Goodwin, you've been very naughty, and I think it's time people found out *all* about it.'

She nodded to Billy and Millicent on the staircase landing above her. They began to open the trunks as fast as they could.

Miss Primly darted out from behind the curtains. Dashing to the stairs, she snatched Dame Biglum's arm. 'Come this way, Madam,' she snarled. 'Your room is waiting, and the doctor said you shouldn't tire yourself!'

By then, most of the trunks were open. The papers inside fluttered and boiled with energy, swirling as they rose like a funnel cloud. An Oculus, far bigger than any Billy had ever seen, ripped open the air above the ballroom.

Miss Primly's latest lie blinked into existence above the storm and flew down the stairway to its author, where it was caught by light from the Oculus and burst in a brilliant flash.

A glowing ball surrounded the panicked Miss Primly. Inside the sphere, the earlier scene replayed itself. Only this time, as Miss Primly mentioned the made-up doctor, everyone could hear her thoughts: *Oh what a delicious lie! I'm so*

196

good at this, perhaps even better than Sir Biglum himself!

The crowd grimaced at this fiery glimpse of Miss Primly's spidery soul.

Meanwhile, the trunks up the stairs continued to rumble and heave. Goodwin's lies and secrets surrounded him in a turbulent swirl. Lie after lie burst apart in the Oculus's light. The first explosion replayed his proposal to Penelope Pennyworth. His thoughts thundered around the room: *She may look like a chestnut mare, but she's saddled with a fine fortune. Once we're married, I'll see what I can do to relieve her burden. All that delectable gold will be MINE!*

Every mouth in the room hung open in shock. Penelope's eyes rolled up to whites as she passed out.

More explosions followed. Glowing scenes unfolded, featuring blackmail, bribery and underhanded cheating. Many included crooked business dealings with his guests. As the scenes played on, the green haze of Greed's piggish features erupted under Goodwin's skin. It clawed in terror, trying to get out.

The remaining trunks smashed open and showered the room with all the lies that had been told in the long history of the manor. Heaps of documents flew at the Biglum family portraits around the manor. Following the fireworks, the ancestral portraits looked less scornful and more sheepish. Especially Sir Biglum II—perhaps the most dastardly ancestor of all.

One last document shook itself free from the innards of a chest and spun towards Goodwin like a pinwheel rocket, igniting the biggest explosion of the night. Everyone in the ballroom ooohed, then leaned forward to watch a final vision through Goodwin's eyes.

He was ten years old and standing in front of the secrets closet with his brother draped over his shoulder. Greed helped Goodwin support the unconscious boy.

Young Goodwin shouted, 'You weakling! Now everything belongs to me, including your name! And there's nothing you can do about it.' Goodwin dumped his brother on the floor and slammed the secrets-closet door shut as the vision dissolved.

The guests shrugged off their shock and fled outside to their coaches. Some feared the supernatural events, others had seen their own dark deeds revealed in the explosions. They jumped into their carriages and ordered them home, leaving all their coats and bags behind. All swore never to return.

During the chaos, Gossip had snaked between each explosion, gobbling up the exposed secrets and carefully avoiding the light of truth. The scarlet manifestation was nearly the size of a barn.

Not far away, the Oculus drifted towards Billy and Millicent as its light finally gave out. The children saw it and smiled at each other, both struck with the same idea.

'Make it a big one, Millicent. It'll eat it up like pig slop,' cried Billy.

Millicent's face brightened. She leaned over the railing and shouted into Gossip's gigantic red face, 'You're right, you glob. I hate my parents. They died on purpose and left me to starve. If not for my lovely, generous uncle, I would have starved too.'

Gossip gobbled up the lies ecstatically, stretching even larger.

Billy looked at Millicent with admiration. 'When you tell a whopper, you don't stop halfway!' He tried one of his own. 'I . . . I never want to see my skeleton parents again! They deserved to be arrested!'

Billy winced as he said it, but Gossip almost burst with delight. Millicent and Billy's lies fluttered unrestrained out of the closet and into the ballroom. As they flew closer, Billy shouted, 'Lean over the railing!'

The lies burned in the light of truth. But the pain was worth it. Gossip was rocked in the explosion too, and shrieked. Its arms shook, eyes and ears spun, spewing rust-coloured gas. Vapour connected with light and burst into a belching ball of flame. The manifestation shrank until it fell to the floor and shrivelled into a blackened slug.

Billy frowned as he dusted the ash off his old sailor suit. Leaning back over the railing, he watched Gossip wriggle away. 'So do you think tonight's ball was a success?'

Millicent leaned next to him. 'A monstrous success, Billy.'

'I was just wondering how we Biglums will outdo ourselves in two years' time.'

*　　　　*　　　　*

Higgins held Dame Biglum's arm as she hobbled up the stairs. At the top, she gasped with relief. Billy and Millicent were each in one piece. Smiles hung on their faces like huge strands of pearls.

Higgins guided her to the children and then

rushed off in an effort to restore some order in the mansion.

'Billy,' Dame Biglum said, hooking her arm through his, 'I was expecting surprises tonight, but not quite so many. My nerves are jumping like fleas on hares.'

Goodwin sat in a heap, muttering to himself. Miss Primly's gibbering was no better. The marble floor and stairwell were black with soot. Singed sheet music, broken champagne glasses and toasted scraps of food were scattered everywhere.

'Well, my dears,' Dame Biglum confessed, 'I'm afraid we're ruined. No one will do business with Goodwin again, I can assure you. But it was worth it. You'll never have to sneak around again. None of us will.'

Billy and Millicent each slipped an arm around Dame Biglum's waist and snuggled against her. The three of them stood wound together and wanting to be no other place at this moment.

'Well, this be a sight more precious than gold!'

Billy and Millicent looked around for the voice.

'Ye have done me proud. I can finally cross over and rest me weary bones.' Pete floated up to them. He hovered high above the dance floor, on the other side of the railing. 'Sorry to miss the ball, but I had to shake that commissioner feller.'

On his shoulder, Jenkins squawked in astonishment at the mess below.

'Pete!' Dame Biglum said. 'We were so worried. We thought that horrid commissioner had caught you.'

'That muggins? Don't fret so much as a fritter. The law's not caught me yet.' Pete thumped his chest and then floated closer, his joy crackling like

200

kindling wood.

'Ah good, that's one less thing to worry about. But there are quite a few others stacking up just now.' Dame Biglum squeezed Billy and Millicent, then turned to go. 'I'm afraid they need my attention. Keep an eye on the children, won't you, Pete?'

'That I will,' he grinned. 'I'll even use me good eye.'

*   *   *

Billy and Millicent were suddenly heaved over the railing. The children fell past Pete's outstretched hand, but an instant later they were yanked up, dangling like socks on a clothes line high over the marble floor.

The commissioner's head solidified around his eyes, then his ghostly body appeared below. 'I'll gladly let them down, Pete—if you agree to come with me. You've escaped my department too long!'

Pete floated up to the commissioner. They were nearly at the domed ceiling, some twenty-five metres above the marble-tiled floor. Pete sheathed his sword carefully. 'Let them down. I'll do as ye say.'

'Pete! Don't let him get away with it!' Billy shouted, squirming.

'Billy! Careful, there, boy!' Pete grabbed for Billy as he drew closer.

'Yes, careful, boy!' the commissioner cut in. 'You've made quite a mess already. Look down there.' He turned Billy towards the empty trunks. 'Your parents will have to answer for that. Every one of the secrets lost!'

Billy looked at the trunks in horror, 'I . . . I . . .'

Millicent struggled to grab his hand.

'Leave those two be, Pickerel, and I'll make no more trouble for ye,' Pete said.

Pickerel began his descent.

All the way down, Billy searched for a way to turn things around.

And then he did what came most naturally.

He told the truth.

'Mr Pickerel,' Billy said, 'there's another chest with a secret much bigger than all the rest.'

Pickerel set the children on the ballroom floor, and Millicent elbowed Billy. 'Billy! How could you?'

'Ye know he can't keep a secret, me girl.' Pete's blue eye twinkled.

'Tell me about this secret, lad,' Pickerel urged. 'It might help your parents' case.'

'It's powerful as can be.' Billy said. He ignored Millicent's horrified stare. 'Pete says there are those in the Afterlife who'd love to get their hands on it. They could probably control the whole place with it.'

Pickerel steepled the tips of his fingers. 'Sounds like I should have a look. For the good of the Afterlife, of course. We don't want it getting into the wrong hands.'

Billy nodded. 'I'll show you where it is.'

'Excellent.'

'If you let my skeleton mum and dad go.'

Pickerel grabbed Millicent by the scruff of the neck and drew her off her feet. 'I don't think you're in a position to bargain, lad.' Then he dropped her like an old sack. Millicent gave a muffled sob as she hit the marble floor bottom-first. 'But perhaps we can work out an arrangement . . . maybe half an eternity. It all depends on this secret chest. I suggest you show me the way.'

'Through the dining room's the fastest way,' Billy said as he absentmindedly patted his pocket. 'Errr . . . I think my brother has the key.' *At least I hope he has!*

Billy dashed to his babbling brother. After fishing through various pockets, he came up with two prizes. He held up the key from the secrets closet and palmed the leather pouch.

'Millicent, you should probably stay here,' Billy whispered, hoping she'd take the excuse to get away.

Millicent looked at him, struck silent by the very idea. She had witnessed some crazy things in this house, but this might have topped them all. She whispered, 'If you think for one second, Mr Billy Bones Biglum, that I'm going to sit here while you have all the adventures, you're as loony as a dodo bird. Make that two dodos and a doodlebug!'

The commissioner insisted that Pete come along too. Billy grabbed a candle and led the small party through the dining room and into the underbelly of the manor.

*　　　*　　　*

Two glowing spectres followed the wavering candlelight and the children's dancing shadows as they trudged through the passageway. Soon they were all standing in the rock-walled room. Several more trunks had been added. 'Look, Billy, Father's paintings!' Millicent cried.

'More secrets?' Pickerel demanded.

'Not the kind that would concern ye,' Pete shot back.

'Yes, the big secret is over here.' Billy took the key out of his pocket and approached the trunk. With his back to the commissioner, he easily slipped the medallion from the bag and lifted the sea chest's lid. 'Have a look.'

'I won't have you sneaking off while my back's turned.' Pickerel pushed Pete to the lip of the chest and peeked in.

Billy frowned.

'What? This old red vase? Looks common as bones on a skeleton.' The commissioner grew more suspicious. 'You'd better tell me what it does.'

And, to Pete's and Millicent's horror, Billy did.

'It can trap spirits.'

Pickerel stroked his chin, then grabbed Millicent and nervously backed towards the cobwebbed wall. 'Show me how it works. With him!' He pointed to Pete.

Jenkins squawked indignantly at the idea of more time in the vase. Pete took his hat off and held it like he was facing execution. 'Go ahead, lad. It's got to be better than Nevermore.'

Billy lifted the vase in shaking hands and aimed the neck at Pete. Translucent strands of colour twisted up Billy's legs and twirled into the vase. Pete's ghostly form stretched forward like he was being sucked into a sewer pump.

Pickerel watched, smiling. 'Thank you so much, children, for leading me to this treasure.'

A wind whistled around the room and whipped Pete's hat out of his hand. Hat and plume were sucked inside like spaghetti, but before the rest of Pete slipped inside, Billy tossed the vase to Millicent.

She fumbled the catch, and the vase almost crashed to the stone floor. But she finally got a good grip and aimed it at Pickerel. He stumbled back in surprise. Hundreds of spindly arms twirled up her legs, reached through the vase, and wrapped around him. A wind whistled around the room as if a door had been opened to an immense and empty place. The commissioner's jacket fluttered madly, his whole translucent body elongated like toffee. He banged to the floor and rolled over on his chest, pointing an accusing finger at Billy. Then he disappeared into the vase with a *slurp*.

'Billy! Millicent! Now!' The rainbow-coloured arms twisted towards Pete, then pulled at every part of the old pirate. His waistcoat and jacket shredded before the children's eyes. Jenkins shrieked in panic and desperately held on. His green feathers popped off one by one. The wind whirled into the vase with a sea storm's force. Millicent couldn't turn it away from Pete. The pull was too strong.

Pete clawed at the rocky floor, but his hands passed right through. He looked into Billy's eyes with a sweet sadness, ready to give up.

The look jolted Billy out of his daze. 'No!' he cried. He jumped forward, and slammed the gold medallion on top of the vase. He and Millicent tumbled into a tangle of cobwebs and rusty chains. The medallion crackled with lightning, then quietened down.

Pete stumbled away. 'That there was a close

one. He closed his eyes, and the shreds of his coat and vest regained their former finery. Jenkins had almost been picked clean of his feathers, but in a few seconds he had a fine new coat.

When Pete opened his eyes, he saw Billy and Millicent struggling to untangle themselves. 'Woulda liked to spare ye from seeing that, Millicent, my lass, but I can see yer as hardheaded as any Biglum. In the long run it'll serve ye well.'

Billy placed the vase in the trunk carefully and slammed the lid triumphantly.

'Well then, you two scallywags, let's shove off outta here.' Pete grabbed for his hat to straighten it, forgetting that it wasn't there. 'I'll miss that cap; she was a fine piece of haberdashery, she was.'

Before leading the way back upstairs, he checked the other trunks in the room. The paintings' brilliant colours filled Pete's misty form with rainbow light. 'Looks like ye got yer treasures back, missy. Bet yer heart's made bright by that.'

Between the paintings and her father's letter, still tucked inside, Millicent had to agree.

Pete rounded up the three trunks and floated them in a parade through the winding secret hallway, all the way back to the dining room.

And that was where they found Dame Biglum, sleeves rolled up and hair a mess. She was busy setting places at the table and fussing with flower arrangements. From the creative placement of glasses, knives and plates, it was clear that she'd never laid a table in her life.

The old woman coaxed one more flower into an already overflowing vase and looked up. She frowned at the cobwebs draped from Millicent's hair. 'I trust you've been taking good care of the children, Peter. They haven't been up to more mischief, have they?'

'These two? Neptune's knickers, no. Just had a small matter to attend to.' Pete chuckled and thumped the trunks on to the Oriental rug. 'We also found Millicent's paintings.'

Dame Biglum smiled tenderly at her granddaughter. 'Three trunks filled with marvels, all from your father's hand. That treasure ought to keep you warm for a lifetime.' Then she grew more businesslike. 'Now come here, you three, and help me finish with this table. All of the servants have fled, except Martha and Higgins.'

Dame Biglum handed the children a fistful of silver forks and made another attempt at the flowers. 'It will be a challenge for us, in this immense old manor, but nothing we can't handle together.'

As the last spoon was nestled into place, Higgins and Martha entered with a splendid meal assembled from the banquet's leftovers. Higgins was more spit than polish at this late hour. His hair was as rumpled as his tuxedo jacket and his tie had taken an anti-clockwise turn. But if he and Martha had been shaken by the strange goings-on, they covered it well.

They served what they had, and as they turned to retrieve the next course, Dame Biglum rose from her chair. 'Higgins, Martha, please. The children can fetch whatever's left. I'd be honoured if you would consider yourselves family from now on. Please, won't you join us?'

A teardrop made rings in Martha's soup as she sat down, and even Higgins's stiff upper lip trembled slightly.

After dinner, they all cleared, washed and stacked. Even Pete lent a hand while Martha and Higgins weren't looking. Billy and Millicent were practised hands in the scullery, so the job was done in a wink.

Once everything was packed away, Dame Biglum kissed the children goodnight and promised she'd be up soon to tuck them in.

As Billy and Millicent rounded the curve on their way up the grand staircase, the candles in the twinkling chandeliers winked out one by one, settling the great hall back into darkness. Billy absentmindedly dragged his finger along the stone banister while Millicent glanced back at the expanse below.

Her smile wavered between satisfaction and wistfulness. 'It feels rather good to have the run of the house.'

'I should say. It's better than a stuffy old closet.' But Billy didn't look convinced. 'Still, I must admit, I miss the old place . . .'

'And your skeleton parents, I suspect.'

'Millicent, I feel awful that I didn't even get a chance to see them one last time.' Billy stopped and turned to cover his tears.

'Oh, Billy! They'll be back, I'm certain.' She smoothed out the flap on his sailor suit with her palms and gave his shoulder a pat. 'Besides, right now you should be rather proud of yourself.'

'Maybe someday I'll feel proud, but not until they're back.'

'Of course. But while we're waiting, I wouldn't mind solving another mystery or two.'

'Well, I suppose you're on to something there . . .' Billy said with a sniffle and the beginnings of a smile.

Everyone was soon tucked in. But not everyone was comfy. After a number of tossed turns, Billy fetched his sea trunk and fitted it with blankets and pillows. He placed it at the foot of his expansive bed and snuggled in. Finally, sleep claimed each one of the heroes and sprinkled them with well-deserved dreams.

CHAPTER 27

THE MORNING AFTER (AND A FEW MORE MORNINGS AFTER THAT)

After the ball, busy days were followed by even busier weeks. Dame Biglum had much to sort out. She knew the family's reputation was ruined, but she had no idea that Goodwin had emptied the family's funds so completely.

Fortunately, it wasn't long before Millicent presented her father's note to Dame Biglum. It mentioned the artwork's great value and its representative in the art world. Just a few days later, Monsieur Henri arrived.

He was a round man in a grey striped suit. The tips of his moustache twirled up and quivered with excitement as he examined the art. Like Dame Biglum, Monsieur Henri carried a silver-tipped cane, and shared her habit of pounding the floor. As they discussed the paintings, one might have thought they were a drum and fife corps, without

210

the fifes.

'Madame Biglum,' Monsieur Henri said as he paced excitedly from one painting to the next. 'While I would love to brighten za world with zese fabulous paintings, it would be a tragedy. No! We must bring only a few to za market every few years. Zis will drive za price and value up. Zat is more desirable, no?'

Dame Biglum was pleased with the plan. She and her cane rapped a most agreeable, 'Yes!'

With an elaborate bow, Monsieur Henri left for the city, where he immediately put the plan in motion. With Millicent's future assured, Dame Biglum needed to address Billy's and her own. Going over some old papers, she discovered Goodwin's factory plans. She was disgusted by his plan to shackle the world to his tea. But the more she thought about it—with a few changes here and a few there, maybe a factory wouldn't be such a bad idea.

Her plan called for a different product, one she had a particular fondness for.

Chocolate!

She contacted Sir Biglum's old team of scientists, and in record time perfected her business plan and a secret chocolatey formula.

The chocolates were wrapped in gold foil and packed in miniature wooden sea chests. She called the sweets: *Billy Bones's Chocolate Doubloons, First Mate Millicent's Bonbon Booty* and *Pirate Pete's Double-Dipped Chocolate Treasures*. She sold them in a chain of sweet shops that were fashioned to look like old pirate ships—with Jolly Roger pirate flags, rigging, and shop proprietors dressed as scurvy sea dogs, equipped with eye patches, cutlasses and fearsome sneers. Parents weren't so sure about the shops at first (particularly the sneering salespeople) but their children were captivated.

Every few weeks, Dame Biglum encouraged her shop owners to hold a contest. They'd hide treasure chests in different neighbourhoods and then supply treasure maps to the town children, who competed to find the chocolate first.

As it turned out, Dame Biglum had more talent for business than all the previous Biglums combined. She was soon running a flourishing chocolate empire. But she never let the success go to her head, as earlier Biglums had. If anything, she, Billy and Millicent led simpler lives. While Dame Biglum put most of her profits back into the thriving company, she also funded schools, libraries, hospitals and parks in the area. She gave her employees generous wages and her loyalty to them earned her theirs in return. Soon the town of Houndstooth-on-Codswattle was thriving as much as the chocolate factory.

*   *   *

With Dame Biglum so busy with her business affairs, Martha and Higgins took on many family duties. Martha looked after the children, but never harshly like Miss Primly. Still, she made sure the children were properly behaved and didn't run around the house like wild savages, unless it was part of a game. Then Martha would join right in and whoop it up too.

Higgins was a wizard at housework. No one really knew how he managed such marvellous meals and found time to keep the gigantic manor spotless. Some guessed that there was a little magic involved. They might not have been wrong, considering how many strange and wonderful things were to be found around unused corners of the old house.

While Martha and Higgins's responsibilities increased, Pete found himself with little to do. All was in order, the villains were gone, and so he mostly retired to the Afterlife. But that wasn't the last of his adventures—far from it. There were old pirate friends to look up, wishes to make, and even though Pickerel wasn't around any more, there were still some shady dealings. Pete dedicated much of his time to cleaning up the Afterlife.

But not so much that he never visited. He returned often to tell Billy, Millicent and Dame Biglum all about his latest ghostly adventures.

And what about Goodwin and Miss Primly? After careful consideration, it was decided there was only one fate truly suitable for both of them— an institution, actually. Marriage.

Dame Biglum set the newlyweds up in one of Goodwin's fleabag apartments and provided Miss Primly with the purse strings of a small annual allowance.

Some might say that they got off the hook lightly, but others might say, after visiting and watching the crockery fly, that they didn't.

*   *   *

As the months passed, Billy and Millicent enjoyed their new freedom, and nowhere more than out of doors. Nature was generous to the children. She

213

provided a riot of greenery and splendid weather for all their outings: picnics, hikes in the fields, and swims in the winding Codswattle River.

One night, the children packed up for a moonlight picnic. They brought cold chicken, bread, a few cakes and, of course, chocolate.

They hiked to a small hill on the far side of the vast lawns and gardens. It overlooked the manor and also had a nice view of the river as it wound like a silver thread through the landscape. They spread out their horse blanket next to an ancient elm tree with leaves that were veined like old sailors' hands.

But before his first bite, Billy heard a sound he'd been half wishing for and half dreading—the rumble of Fleggs's pounding hooves. The wind picked up and kicked the picnic blanket and basket into a heap. A tumble of leaves whisked by and scattered as Uncle Grim galloped across the field.

His cloak of doom fanned out behind him like wings, then collapsed around his legs as Fleggs pranced to a stop.

Billy jumped up. He was glad to see Fleggs, yet still wasn't sure what to think of his uncle. But when he saw Mr Bones leap from Fleggs's back and lower Mrs Bones to the ground, he knew exactly how he felt. And Millicent did too, as her parents stepped through a shimmering Afterlife portal next to the spirit horse.

The feeling was joy—pure, heart-thumping, backslapping, trumpet-blasting *joy*.

Billy and Millicent shouted, 'Mum! Dad!' Billy caused quite a clatter when he dashed over and clasped Mr and Mrs Bones in a hug. 'I'm so sorry! It was *all* my fault!' Tears of relief and guilt fell fast as he hung on, not daring to let go.

'We're back, Billy, that's what matters,' Mrs Bones soothed as she touched Billy's forehead to her own.

'And I never want to hear you say it was your fault again. We can't even imagine an eternity that doesn't include you.' Mr Bones put two shaking hands on Billy's plump arms, then pulled him in for another forceful hug.

Mr and Mrs Hues sped to Millicent and circled round her with a cascade of kisses, finally entwining her in a double ghostly hug.

Billy was drying his tears on his cuff when he felt a gloved hand on his shoulder.

He turned and faced Grim. 'It won't do, you know, to try and take the blame when none is due.' Grim pulled his hood to his shoulder and leaned closer. 'I told you before. If anyone is guilty, it's me. And if not for a few cagey moves by my boss, Oversecretary Underhill, I'd be in Nevermore now.

'Lord Underhill is a master politician, and he was able to wriggle me into a hearing in front of the High Council. I don't think he would have been able to do it if Pickerel had been about. Thing is, the blighter is nowhere to be found.'

Billy tried to hide a grin.

Skeleton eyes may glow soft, but they're sharp at spotting secrets. Grim tilted his head and a curious smile flashed beneath his hollow nose. He continued, 'So it was very lucky he's been, uhmmm . . . detained somewhere and couldn't block the hearing.' He stood up. 'It didn't take long to make the case. The High Council agreed that Pickerel overstepped his authority, and now

215

there's a warrant for his arrest.'

Grim gathered Billy in for a hug. Eternal energy swirled around the two of them, then danced away as Grim swung up on to Fleggs and addressed his brother · and sister-in-law. 'Enjoy your time together with the lad and take care. Someday, a long lifetime from now, I'm hoping he'll be the one that replaces me. Although I see the makings of a master secrets keeper there too.'

Billy couldn't help feeling some pride at his uncle's compliment. He and his skeleton parents watched Grim gallop off to a distant nowhere, then the three walked to the elm tree. By then, Millicent had straightened out the blanket and rearranged the small feast.

For the first time, Billy noticed that Mr Bones seemed a little shaky, and a nasty burn mark extended from his eye socket to his temple. Billy asked what had happened, but as usual, Mr Bones wouldn't talk about it.

Instead, he changed the subject. 'I hope you've forgiven Grim, Billy. Without him, we'd still be rotting in Nevermore.' Mr Bones winced, but quickly regained his smile when Billy nestled next to him.

'It's the talk of the Afterlife,' Mr Hues broke in. 'Been all over the *Eternal Bugle* for weeks.' Then he extended a translucent hand. 'This must be the missing Master Biglum. Millicent has just been telling us about you.'

Before Billy could shake hands, Julia netted him in a ghostly hug. 'Barkley! I'd recognize you anywhere!'

Billy spent the next few minutes sorting out his winding tale. He wanted her to know where he had

216

been for the last twenty-five years, and that he much preferred his skeleton name. This produced another sisterly hug, a few more tears that he'd been through so much, and a promise to call him Billy for evermore.

The Hueses formally introduced themselves to the Boneses, the Boneses to the Hueses, and they were getting on like jam on toast in no time.

The two children lolled on their backs and counted the stars while their parents' conversation washed over them in soothing waves.

Millicent whispered, 'Like I said, Billy Bones Biglum, you should feel proud of yourself. And over there is the final proof.' She pointed a toe towards Mr and Mrs Bones. 'I hope you're finally done with all that mopey business.'

Billy had to smile. 'Well, you were pretty mopey when you didn't think your parents were coming back either.'

Millicent fluffed her hair a bit and replied, 'Yes, but "tragic" looks becoming on me. On you, it looks like a cow pie.'

'Oh, does it . . . ?'

The children traded giggles and rib jabs for much of the remaining picnic.

Soon it was time to pack up and head home. Billy carried the basket. It creaked as it bounced against his leg, joining the muted clacks of Mr and Mrs Bones's footsteps. As his skeleton parents walked side by side, Billy watched them drink in the moon, the stars and the swish of the dewy grass against their bony feet.

*   *   *

Far below, in the sub-sub-basement, muffled shouts burbled from an old sea chest. 'Curse this feather! It never misses a chance to work itself up my nose!'

The fire-red vase heated up a few more degrees. 'When I get out of here, that boy is going to be sorry he was ever reborn. I've a fate waiting for the old pirate worse than five trips through Nevermore. Then it will be my pleasure to take care of you, you stinking, miserable, rat-scrabbled old hat! If I only had enough room to shred you to lint scraps now!' And so, in the blackness of that secret room, the trunk kept rumbling, grumbling, fuming and fussing.

As for the rest of the house, its future was much brighter. The manor developed the much-deserved reputation as the happiest, most delightful and modest home in a hundred miles. Even on the darkest days, its windows glittered with welcome as it graced the hills overlooking the prosperous little town of Houndstooth-on-Codswattle.

ACKNOWLEDGEMENTS

I must start out with a tip of the hat to Luck. She's been perched on my shoulder the whole lengthy process of writing this book. I know, as a manifestation, she should be locked inside my heart, but fortunately for me she decided to take a peek at what I was up to.

In my world (as in Frank Sinatra's), Luck is a lady, and a rather beautiful one. You know: flaxen hair, gossamer robes . . . the works! She looks a great deal like Justice, by the way, except with unimpaired vision. And along with looks, Luck is a clever manifestation. She led me to the host of talented people who made this book possible.

Our first stop was at Writers House, where we met agent Daniel Lazar. With great perseverance, Dan turned this old advertising art director (that's me) into a somewhat presentable writer. It took a number of what we fondly call 'Billy Bones Boot Camps' to accomplish the task—picture yourself crawling on your belly, mired in double adjectives and extra metaphors. Suddenly you're fired on by a barrage of brilliant insights and logical observations. You press on and emerge with twice the skill you came in with. So thank you, Dan. Your swift kicks and deft strokes with red pen are always appreciated.

Along with Dan, I'd like to thank Maja Nikolic, our foreign-rights agent, and her assistants, Matthew Casselli and Jane Berentson. It is also my great pleasure to thank my new friend in the UK, Dorie Simmonds, agent extraordinaire. Everyone associated with Writers House has been a tireless supporter of Billy Bones.

Our next stop took us to Little, Brown and Company in the US, where Luck and I were introduced to our first editor, Amy Hsu. She championed Billy Bones through the many steps it takes to reach an offer. She is responsible for slipping me out of the reading stacks and launching my writing career. Thank you, Amy!

Several months later we met our second editor, Phoebe Spanier. Phoebe is a terrific writing coach and mentor. Her comments and wisdom shine through this manuscript from prologue to final sentence. Thank you, Phoebe, for your faith. Working with you was a delight.

Then, in a most unusual turn of events, Luck and I met our third editor, Nancy Conescu. Nancy is the inventor of 'Billy Bones Cupcakes'. Perhaps you will see them on the shelves one day. But far beyond her culinary skills I owe her a huge debt of thanks for her talented snipping. Nancy's shrewd eye made this book the pacy little tome you find in your hands today.

Around the same time I met Nancy, Luck risked life and limb, braving gales and crashing waves to fly across the Atlantic and introduce me to Rachel Denwood, Senior Editor at Macmillan Children's Books. (I believe Dorie Simmonds and Luck shared a cup of cocoa and a bit of cooperation on this matter.) As I write this, Rachel is defying all the laws of physics and land-speed records to get this book out to our friends in the UK. She must be especially lauded for her bravery in hiring me to do the illustrations. A double thank you, Rachel.

Besides Luck and myself, a number of others

have been around since the start: most notably, friends and family. My friend Gower read the first scribblings multiple times and, before I lost count, my daughter read the book five times. Friends and family, thank you for your support. That goes quadruple for my wife.

I try to keep writing confined to ungodly early-morning hours, but I'm not always successful. There are many times my wife takes up my slack and keeps our family in order. So here I must thank Luck most of all for her special kindness in bringing my darling into my life.

A smart person and good husband would leave it right there. They know that last words always go to the wife. But, as we have already established, I leave a lot to be desired in my husbandly ways, so I will save my final word for you, dear reader. Thank you for picking up Billy Bones. I hope, some day soon, we will share another story.